W9-BUQ-914

RECORD BREAKER

RECORD BREAKER

Robin Stevenson

ORCA BOOK PUBLISHERS

Text copyright © 2013 Robin Stevenson

All rights reserved. No part of this publication may be reproduced or transmitted
in any form or by any means, electronic or mechanical, including photocopying,
recording or by any information storage and retrieval system now known
or to be invented, without permission in writing from the publisher.

Library and Archives Canada Cataloguing in Publication

Stevenson, Robin, 1968-
Record breaker / Robin Stevenson.

Issued also in electronic formats.
ISBN 978-1-55469-959-9

I. Title.
PS8637.T487R42 2013   jc813'.6   C2012-907283-4

First published in the United States, 2013
Library of Congress Control Number: 2012952479

Summary: In 1963, cataclysmic world events threaten to overwhelm
Jack as his family tries to deal with the death of his baby sister.

*Orca Book Publishers is dedicated to preserving the environment and
has printed this book on Forest Stewardship Council® certified paper.*

Orca Book Publishers gratefully acknowledges the support for its publishing programs
provided by the following agencies: the Government of Canada through the Canada Book
Fund and the Canada Council for the Arts, and the Province of British Columbia
through the BC Arts Council and the Book Publishing Tax Credit.

Cover design by Teresa Bubela
Cover photography by Getty Images

ORCA BOOK PUBLISHERS   ORCA BOOK PUBLISHERS
PO Box 5626, Stn. B   PO Box 468
Victoria, BC Canada   Custer, WA USA
V8R 6S4   98240-0468

www.orcabook.com
Printed and bound in Canada.

16 15 14 13 • 4 3 2 1

To Sarah Harvey—fabulous editor, generous mentor and great friend.

One

The world record for rocking in a rocking chair is ninety-three hours and eight minutes, set six years ago, in 1957, by Mrs. Ralph Weir, of Truro, Nova Scotia. More than three days of nonstop rocking! Of course, Mrs. Weir never had to deal with my father.

"What are you doing in my chair?" Dad was standing across the living room with his hat still in his hand. "I've been on my feet all day. Move it."

"I can't," I told him. "I've been rocking since I got home from school. Almost three hours." You wouldn't think rocking in a rocking chair would be physically demanding, but my legs were getting tired already. My calf muscles were starting to burn. Still, I figured I had to be able to rock longer than Mrs. Weir. She was in her fifties, after all. Old enough to be a grandmother.

My father gave an exaggerated groan as he hung his hat on the coat rack inside the door. "Don't tell me this is another record attempt."

Why else would anyone rock for three hours? I wondered. I didn't say it out loud though, because Dad gets hopping mad if he thinks I'm being cheeky, and I couldn't afford to annoy him. I needed his chair for at least another ninety hours. "I really think I can do this one," I said instead. "I can break the record."

He took off his coat and set his briefcase down. "How's your mother?" he asked, lowering his voice.

"Really good," I said. "She was up when I got home from school. And she's making dinner! Sausages." I could hear them sizzling in the pan.

"Thought I smelled something good." Dad's face relaxed into a smile. "You should be helping her, Jack."

"I offered." I rocked more vigorously. "She said I could do this."

He took a couple of steps toward the kitchen; then he stopped and glanced back at me. "You do realize that you're not eating dinner in that chair?"

"Dad! I can't stop now. If I stop now, the last three hours was a waste of time."

"As opposed to what?"

"Huh?" I didn't know what he meant.

Dad frowned. "Pardon. Not *huh*."

"Sorry. Pardon."

"You can rock some more after dinner, if you must. Now come on. Get out of that chair and help your mother get dinner on the table." He headed into the kitchen, calling my mother's name. "Marion? Marion?"

I kept rocking.

"Marion? You know what your son's doing now?"

Mom's voice was soft, and I had to slow my rocking and strain to hear what she was saying. "It's harmless enough. How much trouble can he get into in a rocking chair?"

There was a long silence, and I knew what Dad was thinking about. A few weeks earlier I had tried to eat twenty-four raw eggs in less than two minutes and eleven seconds but threw up after the first seven. Eggs, not minutes. Right on Allan's shoes. Of course, Allan had to go and tell his mom, who told his dad, who told my dad.

"Your sister," Dad muttered. "Sending him that book."

Mom's sister is my aunt Jane. She sent me the *Guinness Book of Records* for my eleventh birthday, which was a year and a half ago. All that time, and I still haven't broken any records.

Mom actually laughed. It wasn't much of a laugh, just a *hmph* with a hint of a chuckle in it, but the sound made me grin all the same. I rocked harder, the chair thumping a soft rhythm on the carpet. Out of bed, making dinner and now laughing: today was a very good day. Mom didn't laugh much anymore, not since Annie had died, but whenever she did, I always felt this sense of relief.

Like someone had lifted something heavy off me and I could suddenly breathe more easily.

"Jane couldn't have predicted that he'd take it like this," Mom said.

"Hmm." Dad lowered his voice, but I could still hear him. "Good to see you up."

I couldn't see into the kitchen from the chair, but I didn't need to. I could picture Mom standing at the stove, her shoulders hunched up all tense, like she was in pain, her hair limp and her face pale above the same old yellow dress and cardigan she wore practically every day. In the old days, she had always sprayed on perfume and put on bright lipstick right before Dad walked through the door.

I used to be embarrassed by how lovey-dovey they were—the way Dad used to kiss Mom when he got home from work, grabbing her and pulling her close, bending her backward as if they were movie stars. He'd put on his Perry Como voice and sing to her: "*Till the end of time, long as stars are in the blue…*" I used to think it was sappy. Now I'd give anything to have things go back to the way they were.

Maybe Mom would laugh again if I broke this record. I closed my eyes and imagined her telling her friends about it: *My son Jack set a world record, can you believe it? He rocked in a rocking chair for three days! What a riot…*I could almost hear the peals of laughter from Mom, the chuckles and admiring comments from her friends.

I rocked harder. My legs were starting to hurt. I grabbed the Thermos from beside my chair and took a sip of water. A very small sip. Peeing was going to be a challenge. I had put an empty bucket beside the chair, just in case, but it wasn't going to be easy to pee into it without stopping rocking. I couldn't imagine how Mrs. Weir had managed it.

"Jack! Come set the table." Dad stepped into the living room. "You can go back to your rocking after dinner, if you really must."

"I can't stop. I already explained this, remember?"

He frowned at me. "Of course you can, Jack. You need to eat."

"The record is for continuous rocking. You can't just do an hour here and an hour there. Otherwise there'd be thousands of old people breaking the record every day. It wouldn't mean anything."

"And it is supposed to mean what, exactly?"

"It's a *record*," I said, exasperated. "It means you are the best in the world at something."

"At rocking a chair? Hmm. And you have to do this for how long?"

"Ninety-three hours and eight minutes. Well, nine minutes, I guess. To beat the old record."

He stared at me. "Ninety-three hours! Good Lord, that's almost four days, Jack. You can't sit there for four days."

"I'm not just sitting," I reminded him. "I'm rocking. It's actually good exercise." I thought this might help my cause, since Dad always wanted me to be more active.

He snorted, and Mom appeared at his shoulder. "You have school tomorrow," she said. "Anyway, you can't stay up all night."

I looked at my watch. "I'm past three hours already," I said. "I really think I can do this."

Dad crossed his arms across his chest. "And I really think you'd better get your backside out of that chair and help your mother get dinner on the table."

"But…"

"Now. And don't you let me hear you arguing with your mother again."

You would have thought he'd want me to succeed, but apparently not. I stopped rocking and the squeak-bounce of the chair was replaced by silence.

I stood up and staggered toward the kitchen. My legs were trembling like I'd run a marathon, but I knew I could have beaten the record if they'd left me alone. When was I ever going to get four days at home without anyone telling me what to do?

Never, that's when.

Two

It felt like the middle of the night when Dad shook me awake. "Jack. Jack."

"What?"

"Time to get up," Dad said. "School day."

It was dark in my room, but the light from the hallway was shining in through my bedroom door. I could hear rain dripping from the roof: the eaves trough was blocked again.

"I have to go to work," he said. "Get yourself some breakfast, and don't bother your mother."

"She's staying in bed again, isn't she?"

He nodded. "I think so. Yes."

It wasn't unusual these days, but she'd seemed so much better last night. She'd even laughed, sort of. I got out of bed and picked up my pants, still lying where I'd dropped them at bedtime. "What's *wrong* with her, Dad?" I asked for the hundredth time.

He didn't answer for a long minute. He stood there, watching me dress. Finally he sighed, a long, noisy gust of air, like something deflating, and said the same thing he always said. "She's just sad, Jack. Very, very sad."

I made myself some toast, brushed my teeth and packed myself a lunch. There wasn't a sound from my parents' bedroom. I eyed the closed door. Dad had said not to bother my mother, but it never felt right to leave for school without even seeing her. I pushed the door open a crack and peeked inside. The room was dark, the curtains closed, and Mom was lying curled up under a heap of blankets in the middle of the bed. I tiptoed into the room and leaned forward, bending over her so that I could see her face in the light spilling in from the hallway. She didn't move. "Are you okay?" I whispered in her ear. Her hair smelled like lemons and stale sweat.

She turned her face away from me, but not before I saw the tear-shiny streaks on her cheeks.

"Mom?" I said.

She didn't answer.

"I'm sorry," I said. "I didn't mean to bother you. I'm going to school now. I'll see you later." I backed out of the room and closed the door behind me.

I usually walked to school with Allan. My dad and his dad are cousins, which makes us second cousins. We'd sort of grown up together, and he only lived a couple of blocks away. It would've made more sense for him to pick me up, because I lived closer to the school, but Allan insisted that we take turns. I'd pointed out that this meant I had to walk the two blocks to his house and then right back past my own, but Allan insisted it was only fair. I didn't mind the actual walking, but his lack of logic drove me crazy.

Mrs. Miller met me at the front door of their house. She was wearing a white housecoat, and her hair was in curlers.

"Come on in," she said. "Allan's getting his things ready. How's your mother?"

I shrugged. "Same, I guess."

"You poor dear."

There was a hard lump lodged in my throat, and I couldn't think of anything to say. It had been almost a year since Annie died, and Mom had been like this for most of that time. On her good days, she got out of bed and tried to act normal, but you could tell she still thought about

Annie a lot. She often had a blank look on her face, like her mind was far away, and I'd have to ask her a question at least twice before she'd hear me. And those were the good days. On the bad days, she didn't leave her room.

Dad always said she was sad, but lots of people were sad, and they still got out of bed every morning and looked after their kids. I knew it was awful that Annie had died, but sometimes it seemed like my mother had forgotten she still *had* a kid to look after. Didn't I count? I couldn't help wondering if there was something else wrong with her, like cancer or something. She complained of headaches a lot, and sometimes she wouldn't eat at all. I had a feeling Mrs. Miller knew more about my mother's problems than I did, and that bothered me. It always made me nervous when grown-ups whispered things to each other. It made me think there was something scary going on that no one was telling the kids about.

Allan and I walked to school in the rain. Allan's house was a big new one at the end of a dead-end street. A cul-de-sac, Mrs. Miller called it. We walked up the hill and past the brick bungalow where my friend David used to live. Before he moved away, we'd played together practically every day. I'd done jigsaw puzzles at his kitchen table, eaten his mom's pumpkin bread and peanut butter candy, played Yahtzee in his bedroom, climbed the old tree in his backyard. I still thought of it as David's house, but he'd been gone for months now. I kicked a pine cone along in front of me as we walked around the bend and on to Church Street. The houses on Church Street were smaller and more rundown than where Allan lived. Mine was the fourth one on the left. I knew Mom was probably still in bed, but I couldn't help scanning the windows as we walked past.

"Aren't you ever going to put the fence back up?" Allan asked. He screwed his face up as if my house had a bad smell.

It was a bit of a mess: piles of wood stacked alongside the house, dead grass and weeds, a mound of dirt still heaped up against the back wall. Dad had pulled the fence down last fall so that the workers could get their machines into the backyard. He'd hired them to build a fallout shelter for us: *Just in case*, he'd said. *Best to be prepared.*

It was the American president, John F. Kennedy, who had got Dad so steamed up about the bomb. Kennedy had said people should build shelters in case of nuclear war. Dad started talking about it all the time, waving around a copy of *Life* magazine, but Mom was pregnant with Annie then, and she said she didn't want to think about that sort of thing. She said Dad was obsessed and that there wasn't going to be a war. "People aren't that stupid," she said.

"Not the Americans, maybe, but you never know about the Russians," my father said.

Mom glanced my way. I was on the couch with a comic book, pretending to read, but my ears were wide open and I was hanging on every word. "Even if it happened, we wouldn't be a target," she said. "New York, maybe, or Washington."

"Ottawa could be a target," my father said. "Even Hamilton, with the steel factories. Besides, New York isn't that far away. There'd be fallout."

Our house in Ancaster was only a twenty-minute drive from Hamilton's steel factories. I imagined the bright flash, the ball of white fire like a second sun on the horizon, the column of smoke rising into a poisonous mushroom cloud, the invisible but deadly radiation being carried toward us by the wind.

"For God's sake, Frank. That's enough." Mom's lips were pressed together tightly, one arm cradling her belly protectively. "You'll give Jack nightmares."

I pretended I hadn't heard. Truth was, I was already having nightmares. Every time we had a drill at school and had to hide under our desks, I'd start thinking and dreaming about it all over again. Would it be better to die right away? If Hamilton was hit directly, we'd be vaporized, like the people in Hiroshima. That might be better than a slow, lingering death from radiation poisoning.

Allan had lent me a book a few months earlier—he'd swiped it from his parents' bookshelf, but they didn't know—called *Alas, Babylon.* It was about some survivors of a nuclear holocaust in a small town in Florida. They managed to stay alive by fishing and farming and shooting the highwaymen who tried to steal from them. We didn't have a river to fish in, or land to farm, or a gun to defend ourselves. Even if the bomb and the fallout missed us, I didn't think we'd stand a chance of surviving the aftermath.

I suppose Dad felt like he had to do something, because after Annie was born, he started planning the fallout shelter, reading government brochures and sketching out designs, calculating how many inches of concrete or steel it would take to protect us from radiation. I guess it should've made me nervous, but the truth was, it made me feel better. We were doing something. Like Randy, the hero of *Alas, Babylon,* we would be prepared.

It was even kind of exciting. Sometimes Dad let me help him, explaining his sketches to me and letting me add columns of figures, because, as he said, I had a good brain for arithmetic. We'd gone out in the backyard one evening and I'd held the tape measure for him while he paced out exactly where the bomb shelter could go. It had been raining lightly, and he was in a good mood, laughing and ruffling my damp hair. That night, with music playing softly and Mom resting on the couch with three-week-old Annie sleeping in her arms, it had been hard to feel worried about anything. We could have been planning a backyard fort, a clubhouse for me and my friends to play in.

And then the Russians put nuclear missiles in Cuba, and it stopped being a game. *See?* Dad had said. *You see? They're going to do it. The crazy bastards are going to do it. But don't worry. We'll be ready.*

Within a few days there was a crew of workers in our backyard. By Christmas, Annie was almost four months old and the shelter was finished. Then, in January, Annie died and my mother sort of fell apart, and my aunt Jane came all the way from England to look after her for a few weeks. Mom cried all the time, which was awful, but after Jane left, it was even worse. Half the time, Mom wouldn't even get out of bed. I started having nightmares again, and sometimes Annie would be in my dreams too, crying and sick from radiation poisoning, or dead and buried in the giant hole behind our house.

After Annie died, Dad lost interest in the shelter. I guess he'd been mostly concerned about protecting Annie, but as it turned out, he couldn't do that anyway. So the shelter was basically finished, but there was nothing in it at all—no food or water or iodine tablets or whatever else it was supposed to have. If there was a war, we'd starve to death. I wondered, if we all died, whether I'd see Annie and whether my mom would be happy again. Though if the whole planet was wiped out, maybe heaven and hell would be gone too. Could heaven and hell go on existing if there were no people anymore? I wasn't sure how that would work. It wasn't the sort of question you could ask anyone.

Three

Our school is called Memorial, and it's on Wilson Street, the main road through town. It's not far from my house, not even a ten-minute walk. Ancaster is a pretty small town. Not even a town, really. More of a village. There's the one main street and on it there's our school, the new post office, Thompson's Grocery Store, Township Hall, the bank, a couple of churches, the fish-and-chips shop and Tony's Variety. And that's about it. If you head west, you're in farmers' fields, and if you head east, you're going toward Hamilton.

By the time Allan and I got to school, we were both soaked. Miss Thomas was standing at the front of the class, and she nodded and smiled at Allan and me. She was the nicest—and prettiest—teacher in the school. She wore pointy-toed shoes with high heels, and purple eye shadow.

It was her first year teaching and she got all flustered sometimes, but hardly anyone took advantage like they would have with some other teachers.

As I made my way between the rows of desks to my seat near the front of the classroom, I felt something hit me in the back of the head. I pretended not to notice. I sat down, took my books out of my bag and placed them neatly on my desk. And then—ever so casually, like I was just smoothing down my hair—I reached back and felt the wet, gummy spitball stuck there. I flicked it to the floor and, without looking around, opened a book and tried to act as if nothing had happened.

My ears were on fire though. Probably everyone sitting behind me could see them glowing, sticking out on either side of my head like two red beacons.

Richard Cole, from whose mouth I was sure the spitball had come, sat three rows back and one row over. I could feel his eyes on me and picture his satisfied grin. Richard was tall—the tallest kid in our class—and fair-haired, with a thin freckled face. We'd been friends back when we were little kids. He lived on my street, so we'd ridden our bikes together and played at each other's houses. We'd drifted apart a few years ago, but it had all been friendly enough until fifth grade. For some reason, Richard had turned into a real jerk. It hadn't been so bad when I'd had David on my side, but this year I was on my own. Grade seven, and still Richard wasn't showing any signs of growing up.

Mom had wanted to talk to my teacher about it, but Dad wouldn't let her. He said I had to fight my own battles. He was right: if the teachers got involved, it'd only make things worse. Mom had no idea about how things worked at school.

Still, it was all very well for Dad to tell me to fight my own battles. He's over six feet tall and big in every way: strong and square-jawed and broad-shouldered. Even his hands are huge. He used to play baseball, and even though he's thirty-five, he looks like a movie star. My parents used to say I'd be like him when I got older, but they stopped saying that a while back. It's pretty obvious that I don't take after my dad. I bet he never got hit with spitballs when he was a kid.

Miss Thomas told us to work on our math problems, and I gratefully lost myself in fractions and ratios. Time passed way too quickly though, and soon enough we were all changing into gym clothes. We trooped down the stairs, single file, and across the field. I saw the bases set up and my heart sank. Baseball.

Mr. Barnes, our phys ed teacher, was standing by home base. He didn't look like any kind of athlete. He was a small balding man with a high-pitched nasal voice, and he always wore the same brown pants and beige shirt.

"Come on, hurry up," he called out.

I looked at Allan and made a face. We both knew what was coming.

"Team A, Richard. Team B, ahh…Cathy. Let's get going." Mr. Barnes adjusted his heavy-framed glasses on his nose and hiked his pants up higher. "No dillydallying! Let's play ball!"

Richard and Cathy took a few steps forward, separating themselves from the group before turning to survey us. I shuffled my feet, digging the toe of one runner into the soft damp grass. I hated it when we all had to stand in a line. Over the summer, it seemed like other kids had all gotten taller and I hadn't. I was really short. Not short enough to be useful—the record for shortness was held by a dwarf called Georges Buffon, who was only sixteen inches tall. I wasn't in that league. I was fifty-two inches: short enough to get teased about it but not short enough to be famous.

"Thomas," Richard said.

Thomas Atkins, a tall, heavy boy who could hit a ball halfway to the moon, stepped forward.

Cathy tucked her curls behind her ears and chewed on her bottom lip for a few seconds. "Pete," she said.

Pete Schultz grinned and winked at Cathy, and a few of the girls giggled.

"Mark." Richard beckoned to a wiry kid. I knew Mark was a fast runner because he'd chased me more than once, to steal my hat or knock my books out of my hand or carry out some other prank.

And on it went, punctuated by occasional groans and stifled giggles, until I was the last one standing there. As usual.

Richard didn't even try to hide his disgust. He actually groaned out loud, then jerked his thumb toward me, scowling. As we walked away to take our positions—he put me in deep outfield, which was fine by me as I wouldn't know where to throw the ball if by some miracle I caught it—I glared at him.

"You're such a jerk," I said.

"You're such a jerk," he repeated mockingly, his voice a high falsetto. "Boohoo. Jack called me a jerk. I'm going to cry."

I turned away, furious, wishing I had the courage to punch him. Sometimes I imagined doing it—imagined the feel of my knuckles smashing into his face—but I knew I wouldn't ever do it. If it came to a fight, Richard would pound me into the ground. Besides, fighting was stupid.

Standing in the outfield, keeping an anxious eye on the ball, I let myself imagine how shocked Richard would be if I broke a record. Maybe someone from the newspaper would come to the school to interview me. I'd be on the front page: Jack Laker, Record Breaker! That would show Richard.

Dad would be pretty shocked too. It bothered him that I didn't like sports. I knew this because I'd heard him tell my mother, more than once. He'd coached the boys' baseball team down by Spring Valley arena when I was younger. I'd played for three whole seasons before he finally gave up in disgust and let me quit. It wasn't like I hadn't tried. I knew how much it mattered to him. I knew how disappointed he'd been in me.

Even though he'd stopped pushing me to play baseball, I felt like I had let him down. Sports were important to him. Even grumpy old Mr. Gilmore next door got Dad's approval, just because he'd been a marathon runner a hundred years ago.

Dad was going to get a real surprise when I broke a record. Sometimes I closed my eyes and pictured his face when I told him: wide-eyed shock, mouth dropping open, then that movie-star smile slowly widening as he realized it was true. *I didn't think you had it in you,* he'd say, shaking his head. *Looks like I was wrong, son.*

I could hardly wait.

Four

After school, Mrs. Miller picked us up in her blue-and-white Ford. "Jack, you're coming home with us. Hop in, boys," she said. Her nails were painted red and her blond hair curled up at the bottom, like Jackie Kennedy's, only a little longer. It looked like little waves breaking just above her shoulders. She was wearing a pearl necklace too. Mrs. Miller was very glamorous for a mother.

"Did you talk to my dad?" I climbed into the backseat.

"Yes," she said. "He has to work late and your mom's had a hard day, so you're staying with us tonight."

"Okay," I said. It wasn't the first time.

When we got back to the Millers' house, I went to the bathroom and stayed there for a long time, looking at *National Geographic* magazines. I wanted to be alone, but it's hard when you're a guest. I could hear Allan and his mom whispering to each other, but I couldn't make out what they were saying. I was pretty sure they were talking about my family though.

Everything seemed so wrong lately, and it seemed to me that the wrongness must show. When I looked in the mirror above the sink, I was almost surprised to see my own familiar face: brown eyes, little-kid snub nose, front teeth too big for my mouth. Same face I had a year ago, before everything got messed up. I wrinkled my nose at my reflection and wished I had broader shoulders. I pushed my sleeves up and flexed my muscles. Scrawny was the only word for me. I tried a few different angles but didn't find any that made me look less pathetic.

Finally I had to leave the bathroom, because I didn't want Mrs. Miller to come knocking on the door and asking me if I was all right. Allan and I went up to his room and worked on his model airplane for a while, and I told him about my rocking-chair record attempt.

"Doesn't sound too hard," he said.

"I could have done it," I told him.

Allan squinted at me from behind his thick glasses. His lenses were blurry with smudged fingerprints and spattered with white flecks. Toothpaste, maybe, or spit. Something gross. "I was thinking maybe your family is cursed."

"That's a stupid thing to say. The stupidest thing I ever heard." But his words were bouncing around in my skull. *Cursed. Cursed. Your family is cursed.*

He shrugged. "Seems like a lot of bad luck for one family to have."

"Not *that* much." My heart started thumping like crazy.

"That baby that died, and now your mom being sick, I mean."

"*That baby* was called Annie. And my mom's not really sick. She's just sad about Annie. So it's really all the same thing, isn't it?"

Allan looked at me, his carrot-orange hair sticking straight up, his cheeks pink under all the freckles. "You found her, didn't you? The baby? In her crib?"

My mouth opened but nothing came out.

"My mom told me," Allan said.

"I don't want to talk about it." In my mind, a door slammed closed, with my memories of Annie locked securely on the other side. "Anyway, my mom will be fine."

"My mom said it'll be a miracle if she ever gets over that baby dying." Allan picked up a toothpick and spread a thin line of glue on the F-16's wing. "She said it's a terrible thing for a child to die before its mother."

I felt like hitting him. "We're not cursed," I said. "You shouldn't say stuff like that." But what if he was right?

"People who lose a child, they're never the same again. That's what my mom says," Allan said comfortably.

I hated the way he always had to tell me what his mother said, but even more than that, I hated feeling like he might know more than I did about what was going on. "Did she say...did your mom tell you what's wrong? I mean, with my mother?"

Allan looked away, his cheeks flushing red behind all the freckles. "Not really," he said.

I didn't believe him. According to our parents, Allan and I were best friends, but we weren't really. I didn't like him all that much. Whenever he thought he knew something I didn't, he would get a smug grin on his face that annoyed the heck out of me. Other than our dads being cousins, the only thing we had in common was that we were both lousy baseball players. It wasn't much to build a friendship on.

My dad always said Allan was spoiled rotten, and if you asked me, he was right. The biggest problem in Allan's life was that he had to practice the piano for twenty minutes a day. I looked around his room: paint-by-number pictures proudly displayed on the wall, model planes hanging from the ceiling on thin strands of fishing wire, stacks of comic books, the smell of glue, the blow-up mattress on the floor where I was supposed to sleep, the plate of Oreos his mother had brought up for us. *A special treat on a hard day*, she had said. Like cookies would help.

I took the airplane from his hand and tossed it, not as gently as I should, onto his desk.

"Hey! Careful. The glue's not dry."

"Let's go outside," I said.

Allan examined the plane carefully, inspecting it for signs of damage. "Okay," he said finally. Standing on tiptoe, he set the plane down on the top shelf of his bookcase—out of my reach—and turned to me. "I'm making allowances because of what you're going through," he told me.

I didn't say anything, but I gave him a look that anyone with half a brain would know meant *shut up*.

Allan shrugged and looked out the window. "Um, you want to go to Tony's?" he offered. "We could buy some candy."

"Okay." I followed him downstairs and stood by the front door while he went into the kitchen to ask his mother's permission. Across the living room, a brand-new television sat on a low table. It was the biggest one I'd ever seen, even bigger than the one at our school, and it was color. I'd never seen color television before. Mrs. Miller had promised we could watch it after dinner. Like the Oreos, this was supposed to cheer me up, but it didn't. Mrs. Miller thought my mother would never be okay again. I knew that was why she was trying so hard, so all her smiles and cookies and niceness only made me feel worse than ever.

Mrs. Miller walked out of the kitchen with Allan at her side. "Jack. How are you doing?"

"Fine, thank you, Mrs. Miller." I made myself look her right in the eyes so she would believe me and stop asking.

"Well, you boys have fun. I've given Allan a nickel for each of you. Don't eat too much though, because I'm making chicken potpie. And be home for dinner at five."

"Yes, Mrs. Miller. Thank you. We will." I forced myself to smile at her. She had fresh red lipstick on, and gold earrings. Allan's mother always looked sort of shiny, I thought, like she'd been polished.

I couldn't remember the last time my mother had worn lipstick or jewelry. She hadn't even worn the necklace I'd given her for her birthday, and that was more than three weeks ago. Since Annie died, my mother had to be reminded just to take a shower.

Five

"Hey, boys," Tony said as we stepped inside his store. Tony had an Italian accent and a big round belly that looked as hard as a bowling ball. He was always listening to the radio while he worked. He turned it down when grown-up customers came in, but he didn't bother when kids did. I'd learned lots of things from Tony's radio—things my parents talked about in quiet voices after they thought I was asleep. Last year, when Dad was working on the fallout shelter, the people on the radio were always talking about what was going on with the Cubans and the Russians.

"Hi, Tony," we said in unison.

"What's it going to be then?"

We pooled our nickels and picked out a bunch of candy—Hot Tamales, which I didn't like but Allan did, plus Atomic Fireballs, candy cigarettes, marshmallow cones and Tootsie Rolls.

"Your mom like that necklace you bought her?" Tony asked.

I looked down at the candy shelves. "Yes, she did, thank you." It had been pretty—gold, with a heart-shaped pendant and a clear blue stone set in it—and Tony had let me have it for half the regular price.

"Bet it looks real nice on her," Tony said. "Haven't seen her in here for a while."

"She's been busy," I said.

"Well, you give her my best." Tony waved goodbye to us as we left, watching to make sure we closed the door tight behind us.

"I heard Tony has cancer," Allan whispered as we walked away.

The air outside was cold and damp, and I shivered. "You did? From who?"

He ignored my question. "That's why his stomach is so huge. There's a growth in it. A giant tumor."

"He's always looked like that." I felt uneasy, thinking about my mom. What if she had cancer? She didn't seem sick like that, but then Tony didn't look sick either.

Allan shrugged. "I'm only telling you what I heard."

"You can't believe every stupid thing you hear." I tried not to think about Tony's big belly. "I'll give you my half of the candy if you'll help me with another record attempt," I told him.

He eyed the candy bag in his hand, then looked at me suspiciously. "What do I have to do?"

"Okay. Well…" I chose my approach carefully. "There's this record that is currently held by two Russians—"

"Russians!"

"Yup. And they've had the record since 1931. And I think we could break it, Allan."

"I'm not eating raw eggs."

"You don't have to," I said quickly. I knew Allan hadn't eaten eggs since he'd seen me eat—and throw up—seven raw ones in less than a minute.

"So what is the record then?"

This was the tricky part. "Face-slapping," I said, and moved on quickly before he could object. "The two guys who have the record now are called Vasily Bezbordny and Goni Something-or-other. I mean, we can't let that record stand, right? It'd be…it'd be unpatriotic."

"But whose face are we supposed to slap?"

"Each other's." I grinned at him. "We don't have to do it hard though. The record is for duration, so we just have to keep doing it."

"For how long?"

I decided not to answer that directly. "Well, a while. But I thought we should do a test run. Say, twenty minutes or half an hour. Because when I did the rocking-chair one, there were lots of things I hadn't thought of. Peeing, for one. And food. I didn't have any food close enough to reach, so that would have been a problem."

Allan looked dubious. "And if we do half an hour…"

"Then we come up with a plan. Write to the *Guinness Book of Records* officials and plan the real thing." I grabbed his arm. "Imagine it, Allan! I bet it'd be in the papers and everything. '*Two Canadian boys beat Russians to set new world record*'!"

"Hmm."

"And the candy," I reminded him. "My half of the candy."

"For the test run? Or the whole deal?"

"Just for the test run."

He sighed. "Okay, Jack. I guess I could do it."

We took the candy and two glasses of water up to Allan's room.

"Sitting or standing?" I asked. "What do you think would be easier?"

"Sitting," Allan said.

We positioned ourselves a couple of feet apart and sat cross-legged on the floor. "So we take turns," I said. "You slap me, I slap you…"

Allan shook his head. "This is crazy."

"Why don't you go first?" I offered. "Go ahead." I braced myself, but the slap, when it finally came, was not much more than a pat. "Allan, come on. You have to slap me."

"You said we didn't have to do it hard."

"Well, harder than that! It has to be a slap."

He bit his lip. "I don't want to do this."

"Don't be such a wimp," I said. "Come on. Do it."

Allan slapped me hard enough to turn my face to one side. I blinked; then I grinned at him. "Good job." I slapped him back.

"Ow." Allan put his hand to his cheek.

"Come on," I said. "Hit me back."

Slap.

Slap.

Slap.

My face was stinging, but we were getting into a rhythm, and I was thinking we could really do this, maybe, we could beat the Russians. Then, as I lifted my hand to slap back, Allan's face started to crumple.

And then three things happened at once. My hand, moving too quickly to stop, made contact with Allan's face. *Smack.* His bedroom door swung open. And Allan burst into tears.

Mrs. Miller stepped into the room, rushed over to him and put her arm around him. She was looking at me, and the expression on her face was not one I had ever seen her wear before.

"I wasn't *hitting* him," I said.

"I saw you," she said. "So don't lie to me, Jack. I saw you slap his face. *Look* at him."

His left cheek was bright red, and you could see the outline of my hand. "I know," I said. "But the thing is, it was for a reason."

She interrupted me. "I don't care what the reason was. There is nothing that justifies hitting, Jack. It is just completely unacceptable."

I touched my own cheek. "He was hitting me too." But I knew my face didn't look like Allan's. Not that I was hitting harder. It's just that my skin is more of an olive-tan color, and Allan's is that pale and freckly kind that goes red easily.

"If it wasn't for your family's situation, I'd send you straight home," Mrs. Miller told me. "Honestly, Jack, I wouldn't have expected this of you."

"He said it would be patriotic. He said we had to beat the Russians," Allan said, sniffling and wiping his nose with the back of his hand.

"Beat the Russians? By hitting each other?" Mrs. Miller shook her head. "Allan, come downstairs with me. Jack, I'd like you to stay up here and think about what you have done. You owe Allan an apology."

I considered trying to explain about the record. But if Mrs. Miller knew about that, she'd probably make us promise not to do it again.

Especially if she found out that the record for face-slapping currently stood at thirty hours.

Six

The Millers ate dinner without me. I could smell chicken potpie and hear the clinking of plates and cutlery being set on the table. I was starving. Also, sitting up in Allan's room by myself, it was hard not to think about Mom. *Maybe your family is cursed.* What a rotten, mean, stupid thing to say. Remembering it made me wish I'd slapped Allan a little harder.

I wondered if Mrs. Miller had really said it would be a miracle if Mom recovered from losing Annie. I hoped Allan had made that up. How would Mrs. Miller know, anyway? She wasn't a doctor.

At long last there was a knock at the door, and Mrs. Miller stepped inside. "Jack, you'd better come down and have something to eat," she said. "I hope you've had time to think over what happened earlier."

"Yes," I said. "I'm sorry. We weren't fighting or anything though."

"Allan told me what you were doing." She shook her head. "Honestly, Jack. I thought you'd have learned your lesson after that business with the eggs."

I followed her down to the kitchen and watched her dish me up a plate of chicken potpie. Allan and Mr. Miller were watching television in the living room.

Mrs. Miller set a glass of milk down beside me. "There you go, Jack." Then the telephone rang in the hallway, and she hurried to answer it. I could hear her talking softly, but I couldn't make out what she was saying. Maybe it was Mom. Maybe Mom was feeling better and she and Dad were coming to get me.

I hoped Mrs. Miller wouldn't mention the face-slapping incident.

I gobbled up my dinner—I was starving—and wondered if Mrs. Miller would offer me a second helping. Usually she did, but she wasn't too happy with me today. Then I thought about Mom and Annie and everything, and it seemed all wrong that I was thinking about food at all.

When Mrs. Miller came back into the kitchen, she was frowning. "Jack. That was your father."

I swallowed a lump of potato. "Is he coming to get me?" I asked.

"Not tonight," Mrs. Miller said. "You can stay with us. Tomorrow's Friday, so I'll take you and Allan both to school, and then we'll see about the weekend. Maybe by then…"

"Maybe by then Mom will be feeling better?"

"Hopefully." She shook her head. "We'll have to see."

My heart was thumping and the word *cancer* kept slipping into my thoughts, burning hot and scary inside me. No one was telling me what was wrong, and that meant it had to be something bad.

Maybe your family is cursed, Allan had said. Maybe he was right after all.

The next morning, Mrs. Miller drove me and Allan to school. I wanted to walk but she insisted, so I slid onto the cold bench seat beside Allan, rubbed a clear patch on my fogged-up window and watched the houses and trees flash past. Instead of dropping us off like she usually did, she parked the car in front of the school and came in with us. She tried to hold both of our hands, but I quickly rearranged my schoolbag and jacket so that I didn't have a hand free. Mrs. Miller put her arm over my shoulder instead and ushered us into the classroom as if we were in kindergarten.

On her way out, she stopped by the teacher's desk and spoke in a low voice to Miss Thomas. I squirmed in my seat. It didn't seem right for the teacher to know about what was going on in my family when I hardly knew anything myself.

Halfway through the afternoon, someone knocked on the classroom door and then opened it without waiting for Miss Thomas to reply. It was Mr. Kirkpatrick, our principal. He was tall and white-haired, with a tidy mustache and beard. We all called him the Colonel because he looked exactly like Colonel Sanders from Kentucky Fried Chicken.

He beckoned to Miss Thomas. She gestured to us to keep working and stepped into the hallway. I figured he was here because of me, and I could tell Miss Thomas was thinking the same thing because she looked right at me before she pulled the door closed.

I sat still, barely breathing, as if somehow I could protect myself from bad news by being invisible. Inside, my heart was flopping around like a fish out of water. Had my mom gotten worse? Could she even have *died*? Maybe they were going to call me out into the hallway any minute to break the news. But surely my father would want to do that himself. Perhaps my father was even in the hallway with them. I strained to listen, but I couldn't hear a thing through the closed door.

I had a crazy urge to get up and run away, out of the classroom, away from the pale fluorescent lights and all the other kids crowded around me. I felt panicky, like there wasn't enough oxygen in the air, or like I might start crying.

"Psst." Allan kicked the leg of my chair. "Psst. Jack."

I ignored him. Whatever he was going to say, I didn't want to hear it.

And then the door opened and Miss Thomas stepped back into the classroom. Her eyes were red and swollen. "I'm sorry," she said. Her voice shook slightly. "I have some terrible news."

I looked away from her, horrified, and stared down at my desk. I couldn't believe she was going to tell me in front of the whole class. My face was burning hot. I closed my eyes and wished I could disappear.

"The president of the United States has been shot," Miss Thomas said. "President Kennedy is dead."

I opened my eyes slowly. Miss Thomas was silent, watching us, tears shining on her cheeks. Some kids were quiet and stunned-looking, and a few started to whisper to each other. Near the back of the room, Richard pushed his chair back with a screech. "No way," he said. "That's crazy." The girl beside me, Alison, buried her head in her arms and started to cry.

I had to duck my head to hide my relief.

Seven

The Colonel decided to close school early, and Miss Thomas sent us home. She couldn't stop crying. As we spilled out into the schoolyard, everyone started talking all at once: "Who shot him?" "Was it the Russians?" "Now what is going to happen?" Alison was still sobbing. "He was so good-looking," she kept saying. Like that had anything to do with it. Besides, Alison cried about everything. She cried during Duck and Cover drills. She cried if she failed a spelling test. She cried when the other kids teased her about her crying. She was a very annoying person.

"Let's go," I said to Allan. I wanted to get away from all the buzzing and figure out what this meant—whether things would all go back to normal and this would become one of those things we would only hear about on the radio at Tony's candy store, or whether this was one of those times the adult world crashed into ours in a way that might actually matter. We walked down the main street, heading back toward his house.

"I guess the Americans will get a new president," Allan said.

I didn't say anything, because it seemed kind of wrong to think about that right away. Anyway, a new president wouldn't make Kennedy less dead. "It's so strange," I said, thinking out loud. "I can't believe someone shot him. Why would anyone do that?"

Allan shrugged. "Not everyone liked him, you know. My dad always said Kennedy was soft."

"Soft? What does that mean?" It was a word Dad had used about me, back when he was trying to make me play baseball, but I couldn't see how it fit here.

"I don't know. Something about the Communists."

"Huh." I wasn't that interested in what Allan's dad thought. I walked quickly, keeping a few steps ahead of Allan, and tried to think of another record I could attempt to break. There were an awful lot that were plain impossible. I wasn't going to be the world's richest billionaire or the world's best lion tamer. I figured bomb defusing was well out of reach too: the record for that stood at eight thousand bombs in twelve years. That guy might have done even more, but then he got blown up by a grenade.

There was a record for lowest income, which seemed like a possibility, since technically I had no income at all except for a measly allowance—less than half of what Allan got. But the *Guinness Book of Records* gave this record to the forty-two surviving Pintibu people in northern Australia, who survived by eating rats and drinking water from soak holes.

I didn't even know what a soak hole was.

When we got back to Allan's house, Dad's car was in the driveway. Allan pushed open the front door and I followed him through. I could hear Dad's low voice coming from the living room, but I couldn't make out his words. Then I heard Mrs. Miller's higher-pitched voice rising above his.

"My God, Frank! It's just so awful. I can't believe it."

Dad mumbled something and then I heard Mrs. Miller sobbing. "And so young," she said. "I can't believe it. It seems so unfair."

I strained to hear Dad's reply, but his words were lost in Mrs. Miller's noisy sobs. "It's terrible," she said. Her words were broken up by gasps. "A woman—just doesn't get over—something like that. And after every-thing she's been through…"

She? Everything she's been through?

My mother. A chill flashed down my arms and down the back of my legs, and I stood frozen to the spot. *Blood running cold*, I thought numbly. I'd never understood what that meant before. I shivered, and all the hairs on my arms and the back of my neck stood on end.

If something had happened...if she was worse... I didn't want to know. Before I had time to think about what I was doing, I spun around and ran out the door.

"Where are you going, Jack?" Allan called after me.

I ignored him and kept running. I ran through the quiet streets, past my own silent house and down the old rail trail that led past the woods. I had a special place, sort of a tree house—well, just a few planks, really. David and I had found it years ago. Someone had nailed three boards to an old willow tree that had fallen down and lodged itself in the V-shaped space between the branches of another tree. All you had to do to get up there was crawl along a long, sloping trunk that was at maybe a forty-five degree angle to the ground. David and I used to sit up there and read comic books in the summer holidays. Now he was living in an apartment in Mississauga, and no one else even knew about our secret place. It wasn't anything so great, I guess, but it was still a good place to be alone.

I turned off the rail trail and followed the hard dirt path, crossing a rough wooden bridge and disappearing into the woods. Then I slowed to a walk. It was cold out, but my back was slick with sweat under my coat and sweater. I hoped Allan would make up some excuse for why I wasn't with him, but more likely he was telling his mom and my dad that I had run off. Sometimes I thought he liked to get me in trouble.

A barely visible track branched left off the main path and I turned onto it, my eyes lifted, scanning for my place…and I saw a flash of red, high in the bare branches. I stopped walking and squinted up at it.

"Hey there," a voice said, and a face appeared from amongst the branches.

A girl.

"What are you doing up there?" I glared at her. "That's my tree house."

"Did you build it? I bet you didn't. It's been here for years. I can tell—the wood's all rotten." She swung her legs over the side, letting them dangle, and bent her head down so I could see her. She had a dirty face and a mess of dark tangled hair above a red sweater. "Anyway, you can't own a tree."

"I've been using it for four *years*," I said. "Me and my friend David have been using it since we were eight." I pointed to the spot where we had carved our initials into the smooth wood of the trunk. "See? DH. That's David Harris. And JL. That's me."

She shrugged. "So?"

"*So* I've never even seen you before."

"We just moved here," she said. She spoke fast, her words running together. "From Toronto."

I rubbed my thumb across David's initials and stared up at her. "You sound American."

"I am. Well, I used to be. We moved to Canada when I was seven. Which was five years ago, in case you were wondering."

She was the same age as me then. "Where do you live?"

She jerked a thumb in the opposite direction of my house. "Over in the new development. Mohawk Meadows."

"Really? How come you don't go to my school?"

"I haven't started school here yet. My parents said I might as well wait until after Christmas, since we moved partway into the year."

"I guess." Christmas was still over a month away. I couldn't imagine my parents letting me stay out of school that long.

"So are you coming up or what?" she asked. Her eyes were challenging.

"I guess," I said again. I climbed up, feeling awkward with her eyes on me, trying not to let my feet slip on the smooth, damp bark. When I was almost at the top, she held out a hand. I hesitated; then I took it.

She gripped my hand firmly and hauled me up the last few inches. "I'm Kate," she said.

Eight

I shuffled onto the boards beside Kate, my legs hanging over the edge, and sat there awkwardly. I tried to leave a few inches between us, but I was still awfully close to a girl I didn't know. I couldn't think of anything to say, but it didn't matter. The way Kate talked, I couldn't get a word in anyway.

"So what are the schools here like? At my old school, I had a teacher who used to get mad every time anyone made a sound. Really. She'd get mad if you even breathed loudly. I'm not joking." Kate widened her eyes until I could see the whites all around her brown irises. "One time, she actually pulled me right out of my seat and made me stand in the hall just for *sneezing*!"

"Wow. Our teachers are—"

"I mean, I sneezed quite a few times. But I had hay fever, so I couldn't help it."

"Right. Of course not. I mean—"

"It wasn't like I was sneezing on purpose."

"Right." I wondered what the record was for most sneezes in a row, and whether Kate could beat it.

"But I bet the teachers are nicer here anyway. Everyone seems nice here so far. That guy at the store? Tony? He even gave me some licorice for free because I didn't have any money."

"He did?" He'd never given *me* anything for free, and I'd been going to his store for my entire life.

"Yup. Three pieces." She grinned widely. "And then, on my way out, I found a dime on the floor, right inside the door."

"Did you give it to him?"

She shook her head vigorously. "Are you crazy? 'Course I didn't." She pulled the coin out of her pocket. "Still have it, see?"

"Uh-huh."

"So you want to walk up to the village with me? We could buy something."

"Nah." I had an ache in my stomach that wouldn't go away. "My friend Allan says Tony has cancer. Because his stomach's so big, you know?"

Kate snorted. "That's stupid. People who have cancer get skinny, not fat. My grandma had cancer and she was skin and bones by the time she died."

"Yeah?" Mom wasn't skinny. She wasn't fat, but she was curvy.

"Yeah."

I felt a little better. "Well, I better go, I guess."

"Why? Do you have to be somewhere?" She looked at her watch. "It's not even close to dinnertime."

"Um…" Everything came flooding back in a sickening wave of awfulness, and to my absolute horror, my eyes started to fill with tears. I turned my face away from her and swallowed hard. "It's complicated."

She was quiet for a long moment. When she spoke, her voice was uncertain. "You want to talk about it?"

I shook my head. "Nope."

"You came here to be alone, didn't you? I'm sorry. You want me to go? 'Cause I can, if you want. I don't mind. Sometimes I have to be by myself, you know. I mean, that's why I come here too."

"Yeah. No. I mean, you don't have to go." I took a shuddery kind of breath and blinked a few times. "I have to go," I said, and I started scrambling back down the tree trunk.

"Come here again and see me." It was more of a command than an invitation. "I'm here all the time. Practically every day."

I nodded.

"Wait!" she yelled after me. "You never even told me your name."

I dropped to my feet at the bottom of the tree and looked up at her. "Jack." And then I started running back toward Allan's house. Back toward the news I didn't want to hear.

"Where'd you *go*?" Allan demanded. He was in the front yard, bouncing a tennis ball against the side of the house. "My mom's pretty mad."

"What'd you tell her?"

"That you took off. What else was I going to say?"

"I don't know. Nothing, I guess."

Allan missed the ball and it went bouncing past me. "Your dad said to send you home when you turned up."

"He went home?"

"Yeah. He said he was going home to catch some sleep."

"Was he mad at me?"

Allan shrugged. "Nah. He and Mom are too distracted. She's still in the kitchen crying over the president."

I caught my breath. "The president? She was crying over the president?"

He walked past me, picked up his tennis ball and looked at me oddly. "Yeah. So? Even your dad was choked up."

Mrs. Miller had been talking about a woman though. *A woman doesn't get over something like that,* she had said. I realized she must've meant Jackie Kennedy seeing her husband get shot, and I felt like an idiot. My face burned and I turned away, not wanting Allan to read my thoughts and know how stupid I was. "Um, did he say anything about Mom?"

"Just that she was sleeping."

I took a couple of steps away from him. "I better get home. Tell your mom thanks, okay?"

And I started to run toward home.

"Where did you take off to?" Dad demanded. He was sitting in his chair in the living room. His eyes were bloodshot and he looked like he hadn't slept in a week. "I've got enough to worry about without you causing trouble."

"Sorry," I said.

He beckoned to me to come closer. "Jack, come sit down for a minute."

I crossed the room and perched on the edge of the couch. My heart was trying to set a speed record of its own.

"Your mom...well, you know she hasn't been herself since...for a while now."

I looked down the hall toward her closed bedroom door. "I thought she was getting better."

He sighed and rubbed his hands across his face. "I did too. She seemed better, didn't she? Getting out more..." His voice trailed off.

"Dad? Is Mom really sick?" My voice caught, and I cleared my throat. Dad didn't like to see me crying. Even when I was a little kid, he used to say I was too old to cry. *Stop babying him, Marion. It's time he toughened up a little.*

"In a way. In a way, I suppose she is." He looked away from me, out the window at the mess in the backyard. "She needs a rest, Jack. Sometimes when someone is very sad for a long time, like your mom has been, they need some help to get better. The doctor's given her some medicine, but I'm not so sure it's helping."

"But physically she's not sick? She doesn't have, well, cancer or anything really bad?"

"No." Dad looked startled. "What on earth gave you that idea?"

I shrugged. "I don't know. So she's just sad?"

He turned back to me and nodded. "She'll be okay. She needs some time. You could help out, you know. Stop pulling stupid stunts and think about her for a change."

I thought about her all the time. Seemed to me that she was the one who didn't think about anyone else. Anyway, if she wasn't sick, why did she need medicine? "Can I see her?"

"She doesn't want to see anyone right now." He stood up and rubbed his face with both hands. "You heard about President Kennedy?"

I nodded. "Miss Thomas told us. At school."

Dad shook his head. "The whole world has gone mad."

I didn't know what he meant, so I just nodded again.

"Well." He gave a long sigh, then lifted one big hand to hide his mouth as he started to yawn. "I'm going to bed."

I sat at the kitchen table and flipped through the pages of my *Guinness Book of Records*.

Just one more try. There had to be something I could do. One measly little thing I could be the best at. It didn't have to be something important. Anything would do.

I took a pencil from my schoolbag and started circling anything that was even a little bit possible. Eating a whole roast ox in less than forty-two days. I could do that, easy—I bet I could do it in a week—but where would I get a whole roast ox? I circled it anyway, just in case. There was someone who'd eaten four hundred and eighty oysters in an hour. That was only eight a minute, and how hard could that be? I hadn't ever eaten an oyster, but I was pretty sure they were tiny. No way would my mom buy me four hundred and eighty of them though. I'd had a hard enough time getting those eggs. But I circled that one too.

Seventeen sausages in ninety seconds! That was *fast*. I remembered the eggs and felt slightly sick, but I circled it.

Maybe I could do it. How many seconds would I have per sausage? I couldn't quite work it out in my head. Less than six though. Maybe five and a half or something like that.

Ugh.

But at least I could get sausages.

Nine

The next day was Saturday, and I decided to get up early and surprise my parents by making breakfast. Sausages. Mom loved sausages.

I was planning to make lots of them.

I pulled on a pair of jeans and a sweater and headed downstairs as quietly as I could. It was still dark outside. I yawned and stretched, watching my reflection in the kitchen window. My hair was sticking up, all spiky and damp, like I'd been sweating in my sleep.

I opened the freezer and rummaged through the contents until I found the packages from the butcher. A dozen sausages…and another dozen. They were fairly small ones. I wondered if there was any rule about the size of the sausages.

A few minutes later, twenty-two sausages were sizzling in two frying pans. Three for Dad. Two for Mom. Seventeen for me. I hoped the smell of·them cooking wouldn't wake Dad up.

I got out a plate and set it on the table. Beside it I set a glass of water and the kitchen timer. Hmm. Perhaps I should cut up the sausages. It would mean less chewing, maybe. On the other hand, it might be faster to pick them up whole than in pieces. Also, I wasn't sure about the exact rules and whether cutting in advance was allowed. Even though this wouldn't be an official record, I had better not risk it. So no cutting.

I counted out seventeen sausages and put them on my plate. A pile of sausages. A mountain of sausages. My stomach twisted. Usually the smell of sausages made me hungry. Not this morning though. The way the sausages lay there in a steaming brown heap made me think of intestines.

Or dog turds.

I swallowed. There seemed to be too much spit in my mouth, and it wasn't the mouthwatering kind that happens when you're hungry.

I felt like I might be sick.

I took a deep breath. Probably I should have let the sausages cool a bit more, but I was worried about Dad waking up and coming downstairs. No way would he have let me do this. I poked one of the sausages gingerly.

It was pretty hot. I picked up my plate and carried it over to the sink. I turned on the cold tap and let the water run over the sausages for a minute. That should do it. I tipped the plate, drained off the greasy water and carried it back to the table.

Ready.

I twisted the dial on the timer to ninety-five seconds, giving myself a six-second countdown.

One.

I can do this.

Two.

I can. I really can.

Three.

Four.

Five.

Imagine how impressed Dad will be if I get in the Guinness Book of Records.

Six.

I held the sausage in my hand. Warm and wet and slippery.

Go!

I crammed half the sausage in my mouth, bit it off and chewed as fast as I could. And the other half. Next sausage. I was doing well, right on the pace. Chew, swallow, chew, swallow. Gulp of water. Third sausage…*Just swallow. Don't think about dog turds. Don't think about dog turds.* I gagged slightly but managed to get the first half down.

I glanced at the time. Almost twenty seconds and I'd only eaten three! I was already falling behind the record-setting pace I needed. I choked down the last of the third sausage, took another gulp of water and started on number four. Bite, chew, swallow. *Faster. Faster.* Number five. Number six…

But halfway through number six, something went wrong. I couldn't swallow. My mouth was full and I was chewing, but it was as if my throat had closed up, and I could tell that if I tried to swallow I would throw up for sure. I looked at the timer. It'd been almost a minute already. I should be on number eleven or something. I wasn't going to make it.

I walked over to the garbage can and spat out the chewed-up meat.

I never wanted to see another sausage again.

When Dad finally got up, I was lying on the couch, holding my stomach.

"What's the matter with you?" He yawned and shuffled toward the kitchen in his slippers.

"Stomach ache. Ate too much, I guess."

Dad sniffed the air. "Sausages?" He walked into the kitchen. "Jack! There're enough sausages here to feed an army!"

"I know. I was hungry." I thought fast. "I thought Mom might want some."

"Not this many. I'll take her a couple though." Dad took a plate from the cupboard and flipped two sausages onto it. "Is there any bread?" He looked lost, as if he'd never been in our kitchen before.

I got up and found the bread. "One slice or two?"

"Two."

I popped two slices into the toaster. "Butter?"

"Sure." Dad turned and looked at me. "You okay, son?"

"Yeah. Can I take her the plate?"

He nodded. "Try not to worry," he said. "It won't help."

I shrugged. "I guess not. But…"

"I know." He gave me a sad sort of smile. "I can't help it either."

I wondered if Dad still thought about Annie all the time. The weird thing was that although the moment I found her was burned into my brain like one of those Hiroshima shadows, I could hardly remember her alive. Annie had died before she was old enough to do anything. I couldn't even remember talking to her or holding her, even though I knew I had done both of those things. Mostly what I remembered was Mom: Mom carrying her around, changing her diapers, patting her back to get her to burp after each feeding. I couldn't even picture Annie herself. Every time I tried, I'd get this image of her lying in her crib like she was that morning, and then I'd have to shut the memory off as fast as I could.

I knew finding her didn't make me responsible for her dying, but it was hard not to feel that way. I was the one who'd had to call my mother and watch her pick Annie up. I'd heard her scream. I'd stood there and watched while she crumpled up like a paper doll, sinking to the floor of the bedroom with Annie in her arms.

I buttered two slices of toast, put them on the plate with the sausages, poured a glass of orange juice and arranged it all on a tray. Then I took it down the hall to my parents' bedroom. I balanced the tray on one hand, knocked and pushed open the door.

The room was dark, so I put the tray down on Mom's dresser and pulled open the curtains. She sat up in bed, the covers bunched over her knees. "Jack?"

"Hi, Mom. I made breakfast."

"Oh. Thanks." Her hair was tangled, sticking up on one side and flat on the other.

"Shall I put the tray on the bed for you?"

"You can leave it on the dresser."

She wasn't going to eat. "I made sausages," I said. Then, impulsively, I added, "Mom? I tried to break a record. I was going to eat seventeen sausages in ninety seconds, but I couldn't do it." I made a gagging noise, hamming it up. Hoping for a chuckle or even a tiny smile.

"Oh, Jack." She sighed.

"You used to laugh about my record attempts," I reminded her. "Remember? You used to think it was funny. Remember when I tried to learn to juggle?"

"I'm tired," she said. "Just leave the tray there." She lay back down and pulled the covers up to her chin. "Please behave yourself, Jack."

"I will. I promise."

"Can you close the curtains? It's too bright."

It was barely even light. "The sunshine might be good for you," I said. "It might make you feel better." I stepped close to the bed and awkwardly bent over to give her a hug. "I guess you heard about the president," I said. Then I wished I hadn't. So much for making her smile. And what if she *hadn't* heard? Dad would kill me.

But she just nodded. "Unbelievable. His poor wife. To see him killed like that. I can't imagine how she'll ever get over that." Her eyes were glassy with tears, and she looked down at the white sheets stretched over her.

There was a long silence, and I knew we were both thinking about Annie. "Are you okay?" I whispered.

Mom didn't say anything. After a minute I crossed the room and closed the curtains.

Sometimes I was scared she wouldn't ever get better.

Ten

Dad spent the morning working on the fallout shelter. He hadn't touched it for ages, but without any explanation at all he headed outside and started rushing about as if the bomb was already on its way. It was sort of scary. I wondered if Kennedy being shot meant that war was more likely. Dad kept muttering that the world had gone mad, and Mrs. Miller had said something like that too.

I didn't understand, but it was hard not to feel scared.

At school, we had drills where we had to hide under our desks. Last year and the year before, the whole school watched a film in the gym that showed how we should protect ourselves from a nuclear blast. In the film, a character called Bert the Turtle survived by hiding in his shell. It was goofy, and we made fun of it at recess, singing the theme song. "*There was a turtle by the name of Bert, and Bert the Turtle was very alert…*" Still, sometimes when a plane flew overhead I would look up at it and wonder if that was the plane that was going to drop a bomb. It seemed like it could happen anytime.

Even though seeing Dad work on the shelter was frightening, I was glad we were going to be ready if the Russians really did drop a nuclear bomb. After I finished my homework, I went outside and watched him carrying cases of water and canned food down the narrow ladder. "Can I help?"

He nodded. "Sure you can." He stuck his hand into his pocket, pulled out a folded pamphlet and handed it to me.

"*Eleven Steps to Survival*?" I read out loud.

"Read it," he told me. "I don't want to frighten you, but we need to be prepared. Same as we are for fires or any other emergency. It explains what might happen if there is a nuclear attack."

I flipped through the pages, trying to skim the words without letting them sink in too deeply. *Blast wave…heat flash…grave danger to life…radioactive particles…* They were words you couldn't let yourself think about too much or you'd go crazy. "I already know all this stuff," I said. "I meant, can I help with the shelter?"

"Not right now, Jack."

"Dad…come on. Please?"

He sighed like I was asking him to raise my allowance instead of offering to help. "Okay. Why don't you walk up to Tony's and pick up a few supplies? Say, two bags of cookies. Big bags. And we need another six cans of evaporated milk."

"Is this to go in the shelter?"

"Yup. There's a checklist in here." He held out his hand and I gave the pamphlet back. He flipped through it. "Fourteen days of supplies. You should choose a few toys to put down there."

I stared. "Toys?" I wasn't six years old anymore.

"Something to do. Something to pass the time."

"Um, I guess I could find a couple of books."

"Great." He turned away from me and headed toward the steep ladder. "I'm building some shelves down there," he told me. "For the supplies."

"Can I see?"

"Go to Tony's. I'll show you when you get back."

It sure seemed like Dad didn't want me around.

Tony was listening to the radio, like always. He shook his head when he saw me. "Crazy times, Jack. What can I do for you?"

He was wearing a blue-and-white pinstripe shirt, the fabric straining against its buttons where it stretched over his belly. Black hairs poked out through the gaps.

I looked away quickly. "I need some milk. Canned milk." I picked up a big bag of Oreos and a box of Vanilla Snaps. "And some cookies. Dad's fixing up our fallout shelter." Too late, I remembered I wasn't supposed to tell people about it. Dad didn't want the whole neighborhood banging on the door when we only had space and food for our family.

All Tony said was, "No candy for you today?"

I shook my head. On the radio, a reporter was talking about Kennedy. I picked up the cans of milk and put them on the counter beside the cookies. "That's it."

Tony took my money and handed me back some change. "You take care now."

I ran all the way home, my bag bouncing against my leg with the weight of the canned milk, my heart thumping. What if I wasn't at home when the bomb got dropped? What if I was at school? If the bomb was dropped in Ottawa, say, or in New York, how long would it take for the fallout to get here?

I didn't want to wait crouched under my desk like Bert the Turtle.

Dad was in the shelter when I got back. I could hear him hammering, a steady *thump, thump* coming from underground.

I backed carefully down the ladder. "Dad?"

"Hi, Jack. Careful—watch those planks."

I stepped over the wood planks piled on the concrete floor. "Wow. You've done a lot."

"Mmm-hmm."

I looked around. The shelter was small and dim, lit only by the pale shaft of sun slanting in through the open hatch. Dad had put in a set of wooden shelves along one wall. I put the canned milk and cookies down on the floor beside them.

"The beds will go here," Dad said, gesturing to where he'd chalked lines on the floor and wall opposite the shelves. "Bunks. Your mother and I here, you up above."

"Doesn't leave much floor space," I said.

He grunted. "Not supposed to be luxurious, Jack. Supposed to keep us alive."

I couldn't imagine being locked in here, waiting, knowing that most of our friends and neighbors would be dead or dying, wondering who had survived. Wondering if anyone would be there when we emerged. The shelter felt like a grave to me. All I wanted was to climb back up the ladder into the daylight. "Um, I should go," I said. "Lots of homework." And I climbed, my heart thumping, palms slippery-wet on the wooden ladder.

Once I was back in the house, I didn't feel much better. The closed bedroom door kept tugging at me. I knew Mom didn't want to see me, or anyone else for that matter. *Don't bother your mother,* Dad was always telling me. As if I didn't know that. Still, sometimes I'd find myself standing by her door, listening for any signs of life. Sometimes I wanted to burst in and scream at her to get up, get out of bed, and pay some attention to me for a change.

I almost hated Annie for dying. I knew it wasn't her fault, but if it weren't for her, Mom would be her old self. Playing board games with me, laughing at my stupid jokes, putting on records and dancing with Dad in the living room. It would've been easier if Annie had been born dead—if we'd never had those months of getting to know her. Or if she'd never been born at all. What was the point in her being alive if she was just going to die anyway?

Eleven

On Sunday, the Millers called and invited me to come over for lunch when they got home from church. I could tell it was Mrs. Miller's idea, not Allan's, but Dad accepted without even asking me if I wanted to go. I walked over at noon, wishing I could go to the woods and look for Kate instead.

Mrs. Miller said we could watch their new television while we ate. It was nice of her, but all that niceness made me nervous. Even Mr. Miller patted me awkwardly on the back before sitting down on the couch beside Allan. Allan made a point of telling me he was glad I came over because it meant he was allowed to skip his piano practice.

His mom brought our food into the living room: hot meals in tinfoil trays. Having a color TV wasn't nearly as great as I'd thought it would be, since it turned out that the broadcast was in black-and-white anyway. Everything on television was about the president. Kennedy, I mean, not the new one. Someone had been arrested for the shooting—Lee Harvey Oswald, a small, narrow-faced man with dark hair above a high forehead. Allan said that he was probably a Communist, but Mr. Miller said we didn't know that for sure.

It was still hard to believe that Kennedy was actually dead. I took a mouthful of mashed potato and wondered if Mrs. Miller would start crying again. Then I wondered if my own mother was as upset as Allan's mother was. I couldn't imagine it. After all, it wasn't as if we knew Kennedy personally.

They were showing a picture of the White House, and the reporter was talking about the president's body being moved to the Capitol rotunda. "Tomorrow there will be a final hour for the public to pay their respects to the president before the president leaves Capitol Hill for the last time," he said. "The last soldier—" He broke off in midsentence, as if he was listening to someone or something, then started talking again. "We are now switching to Dallas, where they are about to move Lee Oswald and where there is a scuffle in the police station…"

"Why do you think he did it?" I wondered out loud. "I mean, do you think he is crazy or something?"

Mrs. Miller shook her head and shushed me. "They're taking him to jail."

"Isn't he in jail already?"

She gestured at the screen. "Police station. Shh. Listen."

The screen was filled with men, all shoulder to shoulder, crowded together: grey-suited men jostling and pushing in front of the news cameras.

"Where is he?" Allan said. "Where's Oswald?" His dinner tray was balanced on his lap, and he held his fork halfway to his mouth, a lump of steak dangling precariously from its tines.

The camera swung around and people moved in front of it. I couldn't tell what was going on. "He's shot…he's been shot. Oswald has been shot," the reporter said.

"My God." Mrs. Miller's hands flew to her mouth.

The reporter seemed as confused as we were, and it was hard to tell what was going on. Bodies moved here and there—reporters, police—and someone said something about pandemonium, and someone asked someone else if Oswald had been shot, and someone said he'd heard a gunshot and that Oswald had clutched his stomach.

"Did he just get *murdered*?" Allan's eyes were wide. "On *television*?"

Mr. and Mrs. Miller both looked at us as if they had just remembered we were there. "I think you two have seen enough," Mr. Miller said firmly. "You two go play outside."

"But Dad!"

"Go on. Now." On the screen, the confusion continued.

"Fine," Allan said. "Go ahead and make us miss the most exciting thing ever."

"Allan." Mrs. Miller frowned. "Listen to your father."

Mr. Miller shook his head. His eyes were glued to the screen, and he'd already forgotten us. As we trudged as slowly as possible toward the door, I could hear him muttering to himself. "Madness. Madness. What is the world coming to?"

We shrugged on our winter coats and headed outside. It had turned into winter overnight, the sky a heavy leaden grey, a thin frost still lingering on the grass. I took a deep breath and felt the air crackle in my nostrils. I should probably have been upset about seeing—well, almost seeing—someone killed, but it didn't feel very real. Besides, that man had shot the president, so it was hard to feel too bad about him being dead.

"I can't believe they won't let us watch it," Allan said.

"Well, we saw the best part anyway," I said.

Allan buried his hands in his pockets. "They probably would've let me watch it if you weren't there."

"I doubt it," I said.

He gave me a knowing look. "They worry about you. You know, mentally. Because of your mother."

"Allan?" I said. "Go to hell."

His mouth dropped open and hung there, fish-like. "Did you just say what I thought you said? Because I've been a good friend to you. In your, your—your time of need."

I felt like shaking him. "You know what?" I said. "I'm tired of listening to you repeating everything your mother says." For some reason I remembered the girl in my tree house. Kate. "I'm going for a walk," I said abruptly.

"Where are you going?"

"None of your beeswax," I said. Allan didn't know about my tree house or about Kate, and I wasn't going to tell him.

Twelve

She probably won't be there, I told myself as I walked. Sunday afternoon...she was probably at home with her family, or with other friends. Though maybe she hadn't had time to make too many friends yet, since they'd just moved here.

But when I got close enough, I could see a flash of red high up in my tree.

"Kate!" I called out.

No answer. I waited for a moment. Everything was still and quiet, and I could feel the chill of the cold ground through the thin soles of my sneakers. Kate wasn't there. So what had I seen in the tree? I half walked, half ran to the tree and scrambled up, the slippery bark cold and damp under my bare fingers. And there it was: Kate's red sweater, lying in a heap on the wooden planks.

It was all the excuse I needed. I picked it up, slithered back down the tree and started walking in the direction of the new houses over at Mohawk Meadows.

I stood in front of a big brick house, shifting from one foot to the other. I should have worn my boots: my shoes were soaked from the wet grass, and my toes ached from the cold.

There were six houses in the new development. I knew Kate lived in one of them, but I didn't know which was hers. One looked empty, though, and another had a tricycle out in front. For some reason, I thought Kate was an only child, so that left four.

I took a few steps toward the door of the nearest house, then stopped. Kate might think it was awfully strange for me to show up at her house. I was still standing there, sort of paralyzed with indecision, when the front door flew open and someone came bursting out.

Wild curly hair springing out from under a red wool hat, a puffy pink jacket, laced-up boots. Kate.

I waved tentatively.

"Hey! Jack? What are you doing here?" She bounded toward me. She moved like gravity was barely holding her down, like she had springs in her boots. "Did you come to see me?"

I had a big goofy grin on my face. "Yeah, sort of. I guess so. I mean, I found your sweater."

"I'm always losing things. Mom says I'd lose my head if it wasn't screwed onto my shoulders. My grandma made this sweater, you know. It's my favorite." She took it from me, making a face. "Ugh, it's wet."

"Uh, yeah. I'm sorry. It was in the tree…"

"I wasn't blaming you, silly. Anyway, now I'm glad I left it behind. I was hoping I'd see you again."

"You were?"

"Yes. I've been thinking about you."

"You have? Why?" I thought about the last time I'd seen her, and how upset I was. I couldn't have been very good company.

"You seemed so worried. What was wrong, anyway?" She stopped speaking and put her hand over her mouth. "Sorry. I shouldn't have asked that. Bad habit. My mom says everything that comes into my head goes flying straight out my mouth. She says I should learn to think before I speak. Actually, she says I should just talk half the amount I do, and then I'd put my foot in my mouth only half as often."

I waited for her to take a breath; then I jumped in quickly. "It's fine. Really. I don't mind." It seemed to me that most people thought too much before they spoke. Adults especially. They weighed every word, decided what to

share and what to keep secret. They presented information in such a tidy package that you couldn't ever trust it
was true.

Kate looked at me thoughtfully. "I was going to go
for a walk. Do you want to come with me? Or did you
want to come in? You could meet my parents. They're
just doing the crossword puzzle from yesterday's paper.
They're both terrible at them. They'd probably like help."

"Maybe later," I said. "Let's walk. There's something I
want to talk to you about. Something I want your help with."

"Okay. Let's go, then."

Kate walked as fast as she talked. I had to jog a bit to
stay beside her. She kept up a steady flow of chat, telling
me about her old school and her new bedroom and
asking me questions without waiting for answers. Which
was just as well, as I was too out of breath to say much.

"Tree house?" she asked.

I nodded. "Sure."

The woods were quiet and cold, and something about the
quietness seemed to affect Kate, because she suddenly
stopped talking and slowed her pace, walking beside me
in silence. I kept thinking about the Millers. I hoped Allan
wouldn't tell his mom that I'd taken off. If Mrs. Miller
called Dad, that'd be one more thing for him to be mad
about. Maybe they'd assume I'd gone home.

It was only yesterday that I'd promised Mom I'd behave. I shoved my hands deep into my coat pockets and tried not to think about it. It wasn't like I was doing anything wrong. Besides, Dad shouldn't have accepted the invitation without asking me. I kept telling him I didn't even like Allan.

We scrambled up the slippery trunk, me ahead of Kate. Once I was sitting on the smooth wood boards, I pulled the *Guinness Book of Records* out of my bag.

"Here," I said, handing it to Kate. "I want to break a record."

She took the book from me with her dark eyebrows raised. "To get your name in here? I mean, in the next one?"

"Yes. No." I shook my head. "I don't care about being in the book. As long as I break a record—that's the important part."

Kate flipped through the book. "Um, tallest mountain…"

"You need the section on human achievements." I reached over and opened the book to the right spot.

"Wow." She scanned the entries. "Pole squatting! Did you read this one?"

I'd read all of them, many times. "Yeah. Maurie Rose Kirby. The girl who sat on top of a pole for, like, two hundred days."

"To protest being called a juvenile delinquent!"

"I know. Crazy, huh?"

"I think it's great." She turned a few pages. "Ooh. Gun running! And human cannonball!"

I frowned. "Not really options, Kate."

"I suppose not." She sounded regretful. "Wow," she murmured. "This guy got the record for returning the most money. He found two hundred and forty thousand—"

I cut her off. "I know. Almost a quarter of a million dollars. Can you imagine?"

"And he returned it to its owner!" Kate shook her head slowly.

"Well, I know what you'd do," I said. "You didn't even return the dime you found at Tony's."

"Hmph," Kate snorted, sounding a little offended. "It says here that the guy who returned the money got lots of letters from people who thought he was crazy."

"Maybe he was just a really honest person," I said. "Unlike some others."

Kate ignored my dig. "Well, what would you do? Would you rather break the record or keep the money?"

I thought about it for a minute. My parents worried about money sometimes, I knew that. But would a quarter of a million dollars be enough to make my mom smile again? Would her son being a record breaker be enough? "It's not a problem I'm likely to have," I said at last.

"Sounds like something my dad would say." Kate made a face. "Hey, how about this one then, Mr. Picky? Longest fall without a parachute."

"That's the guy whose plane was on fire, right?"

"Eighteen thousand feet! And he didn't even break a bone. Maybe you could do that."

I glared at her. "Ha ha."

"Not funny?"

I made a face. "Okay, sort of funny."

She poked her fingers into my cheeks and pulled the corners of my mouth upward. "There, that's better. You gotta smile at my jokes, Jack."

"You're crazy." I gave her a halfhearted grin.

"Atta boy. You still got a ways to go, but that's an improvement."

I closed the book, tapped on its cover and sighed. "The problem is, a lot of these records are impossible for a kid to do. And most of the ones that aren't impossible I've already tried and failed at." I told her about throwing up raw eggs, which made her laugh, and about the rocking chair and the sausages and the face slapping.

"And his mom walked in? That was bad luck." She laughed and laughed. "I wish I'd seen your face." She made a horrified face: O-shaped mouth, eyebrows raised and eyes stretched. "Hah. You have to admit, it's pretty funny."

I grinned reluctantly. "I guess it is, sort of. But my dad doesn't think so. Or even my mom anymore."

"Mmm. Right." She tugged on a stray curl poking out from beneath her hat. It boinged back into a spiral when she let go of it. "I bet I could do the sausages. Or the eggs."

She swung her legs back and forth like she was on a swing and trying to go higher. "I can eat tons."

"Yeah, but it's harder than it sounds. Really. I can eat a lot too, but trying to do it that fast is different."

"I guess." She didn't sound convinced.

"Anyway, it doesn't help me if *you* break a record. It has to be me that does it."

"Why? Someone call you a juvenile delinquent?" She laughed.

"No."

"You think people will be impressed, right? Kids at school?"

Kids. Richard. Dad. But I didn't say it out loud. "No. I dunno."

Her eyes narrowed. "They pick on you? Call you names and stuff?"

I shook my head. "Nah. Well, one kid does, sometimes, but I don't really care. He's a jerk."

She stopped kicking her legs and turned to look at me. "So how come this is so important to you?"

"I don't know. I just had this idea…"

"Tell me. Please?" Her eyes were solemn, all traces of laughter gone.

"You'll think I'm weird."

Kate started kicking again. "I already think you're weird. All the people I like are weird. That's better than boring, right?"

"I guess." I stared down at my feet dangling in the air. One of my shoelaces had come untied. Twenty feet below, the ground was covered with dead leaves, brown and shiny-wet. "I guess it all started with Annie."

She frowned. "Who's Annie?"

"She was my parents' baby. Um, my sister. She died almost a year ago." I didn't say that I found her.

"Wow. That's awful." She opened her mouth to say something; then she changed her mind and closed it again.

"What?" I asked, feeling oddly defensive.

"Nothing. That's just sad, is all."

"I know what you were going to say."

"What, then?"

I kicked the back of one foot with the toe of the other. "What's it got to do with the record thing. Right?" I didn't wait for an answer, just took a deep breath and plowed on. "Okay. I had this idea. My friend Allan—well, he's only sort of my friend—he said this thing about us being cursed."

Kate's eyes widened. "That's stupid. You don't really believe it!"

"No! Of course not. But a lot of bad things have happened in my family, and I had this idea. I thought that maybe if I could…" I trailed off. "I told you it was stupid."

"You said weird, actually. Not stupid." She looked at me, head tilted to one side.

"Well, it's both." And I felt both weird and stupid for admitting it. "The thing is, I don't believe it exactly, but I can't stop thinking about it all the same. And besides, Mom used to laugh like crazy over me trying to break records. She used to tell her friends about it; she said it cracked everyone up. But lately…" I shrugged. "It keeps getting me in trouble. Dad's furious, and he says it worries Mom…and she won't even get out of bed hardly."

"Why not? What's wrong with her?"

I shrugged my shoulders. "Dad says she's just sad."

Kate didn't say anything for a long time, and I wondered what she was thinking. Finally she sighed. "If I say something, do you promise not to get mad?"

"Sure."

"I mean it. You have to promise."

I looked at her apprehensively. "Okay. I promise."

Kate folded her arms across her chest and tucked her bare hands into her armpits. "Here's the thing, Jack: Your dad's right. Breaking a record isn't going to help your mom."

"I know that," I said defensively.

"Then why do you keep trying to do it? You said yourself it's making things worse."

I shrugged. I shouldn't have told her anything.

"Why don't you think about your mom for a change? Do something that might actually help her?"

I scowled. "Easy for you to say. How do you help someone who won't even get out of bed? I don't think she even wants to feel better."

Kate narrowed her eyes. "You sound mad. Are you mad at me? I'm only saying what I think. Anyway, you promised not to get mad."

I shook my head. Tears were prickling my eyes, and my throat was closing up. "Dunno."

"Or are you mad at her?"

"Not her fault," I said.

"I know, but still..."

I didn't say anything.

Kate sighed. "Well, there has to be something we can do." She was frowning so hard she looked almost fierce.

I liked that she'd said *we*. "Maybe I could find a different kind of record," I said. "You should have seen my mom when I was trying to learn to juggle. Annie was a newborn and Mom was really tired, but it always used to make her laugh."

She shook her head. "Yeah. *Used* to, Jack."

I blinked back sudden tears. "The cold's making my nose run," I said, wiping my face quickly on my sleeve. "So what do you think I should do, then?"

"Hmm. I don't know yet. But I'll help you figure it out," Kate said.

I couldn't exactly see how she could, but having someone on my side felt good. Like the feeling you get after you've eaten your favorite meal or snuggled down in bed on a chilly night: sort of full and warm inside.

Kate untucked her hands from her armpits and blew warm foggy breath on her pink fingers. "How mad would you be if I told my mother about all this?"

"Your mother?" I echoed.

She wrinkled her nose, cheeks pink. "She's good at helping people. Better than me."

"I don't need help," I said stiffly.

"Not you, dumbo. Your mother."

I couldn't argue with that. I slipped my mittens off and handed them to Kate. "Here. You can borrow these," I told her.

"Really? You're sure? Wow. Thanks. I lost mine somewhere." She slipped them on. "Mmm. They're even warm. So, you'll come over after school tomorrow, okay? And you can meet my mom."

With Kate, it always seemed easier to agree. "Okay," I said.

Thirteen

I walked home, not bothering to go past Allan's place. Dad was in the kitchen making spaghetti. I didn't know he knew how. I kicked my shoes off and peered down the hall. The bedroom door was closed.

"She got up for a couple of hours," Dad said softly. "Had a bath. Watched some television."

"Good." I wondered if she'd gotten up on purpose when I wasn't home. Maybe she didn't want to see me. I'd never admit this to Dad, but sometimes I wondered if Mom blamed me because I was the one who found Annie. I looked at the trees outside the kitchen window. The leaves were dry and brown, barely clinging to the branches. Scatterings of them drifted to the ground with each gust of wind. "Did you see the news?" I asked, needing to change the subject.

"No. But I heard what happened," Dad said. "Mrs. Miller called and told me you and Allan were watching. She said you left early."

"Yeah."

Dad shook his head. "Right on television. I'm sorry you saw that, Jack."

I wiped the back of my hand across my eyes roughly. Dad didn't like crybabies.

"Seeing someone killed…What is the world coming to?" Dad's voice was gruff. "I don't blame you for being upset."

I nodded. It was easier to let Dad think that was why I was crying than to try to explain. Especially since I didn't really understand it myself. Since Annie died, I didn't understand much at all.

Annie had been a regular-size baby, but she'd seemed pretty small to me when Mom and Dad brought her home from the hospital. I could cup her whole head in the palms of my hands, and her fingernails were the tiniest little things, transparent and so small they were barely even there. She had long fingers, though: everyone used to comment on it, saying she'd be a good piano player someday.

I had been surprised when my parents told me they were going to be having a baby. I was ten years old and used to being an only child. I wasn't sure I liked the idea of a baby joining the family, especially when I overheard my dad joking with Allan's dad that he might get his base-ball player after all.

But when Annie came home, all wrapped in blankets with a startling shock of black hair sticking out the top, I couldn't help being excited. Somehow it hadn't occurred to me that this baby would actually be not just a baby but a particular person—a little girl with long fingers, a girl who liked to be held facing forward so she could see where she was going, a girl who was so determined to hold her head up that when I held her against my chest, her head would thud against me over and over and over again as her neck muscles strained, then gave out. She was no quitter.

The day she died was just an ordinary Saturday. Annie wasn't sick or anything. Her crib was in the little room between my parents' and mine, the room we had always used as a spare room and games room and office. Mom had put her down for a nap. Mom was fanatical about her not being woken up. If Annie was asleep, I wasn't allowed to listen to the radio or play ball outside with David or the other neighborhood kids or even talk above a whisper. I definitely wasn't supposed to go into her room during naptime. But that day I was working on a map for school—carefully outlining all the provinces in different colors—and the tip of my red pencil crayon broke halfway through Quebec. So I needed to get the pencil sharpener from the desk, which was still in her room.

I turned the handle, very slowly and carefully, and pushed the door open. The new beige carpet was thick and plushy under my bare feet. I held my breath, tiptoed to the desk, lifted the pencil sharpener. The room was dead silent; Annie wasn't stirring. I turned and glanced at her crib as I stepped toward the door. She was lying on her tummy like she always did, her head turned toward me, the pale yellow quilt draped across her small body, her chubby arms stretched out as if she was reaching for something in her sleep. She looked fine. And yet...

I don't know what made me hesitate. Maybe something about the silence in the room, or the stillness of her face. The way, even though I was holding my own breath, I couldn't hear hers. I stepped closer to the crib, not really worried, just watching her face and waiting for the rise and fall of her back, or the twitch of a finger. I wasn't going to wake her—Mom would be furious if I did— but I wanted to see her sigh and turn her head, or kick a sleeper-covered foot out from under the quilt. Because something wasn't right.

I leaned over the white crib railing. "Annie," I whispered. Her eyes were closed, lashes dark and silky against the pale skin of her cheek, her lips slightly parted and her dark hair thinner than when she was born. I reached over the rail and brushed my fingers lightly against her arm. It felt cold. I pulled the covers up to her shoulders. "Annie," I whispered again. "Annie."

She didn't move.

A weird electric feeling was buzzing somewhere around the base of my skull, sending sharp tendrils of fear tingling down my spine. I glanced toward the door, half hoping and half fearing that my mom would walk in. Maybe I should go and get her. Probably Annie was fine though, and I was being crazy, and besides, I wasn't supposed to be in here. I looked at Annie, lying there so still. "Wake up!" I hissed. I pinched her arm, just gently through the quilt, but she still didn't move.

I pinched harder.

Nothing.

I shook her shoulder roughly, my heart beating hard. Annie felt all wrong. Not floppy or stiff. Just—wrong.

I bent close to her, put my hand in front of her face. Touched her lips.

She wasn't breathing.

My first instinct was to run. Out the door, out of the house. Go for a walk. Come home in a few hours. Maybe if I did that, somehow this would not have happened. It would un-happen. It would not count. I took a few steps toward the door—

And Mom came flying through it, almost running into me. "Jack! My God, what is it?"

And then I realized I was screaming.

"Annie," Mom said. She pushed past me, ran the few steps to the crib. "Annie? Jack, what is it? What—"

She broke off, staring down at Annie. I followed her gaze, hoping that Annie would wake and start to cry—half expecting her to; surely I'd been wrong—but she didn't stir. Mom bent and lifted her up. "Annie? Annie! Annie!" She was shaking her, and still Annie didn't wake, and my mother sank to the floor with the baby still in her arms, screaming for my father.

I felt as if I was invisible.

And I felt as if it was my fault. I knew logically that if I hadn't gone in, sooner or later Mom would have gone to check on her and found her. I knew that. But ever since Annie died, I couldn't stop thinking that if I hadn't gone into her room, maybe she would have woken up like she always did.

If that red pencil hadn't broken.

If I'd outlined Quebec in green instead of red.

Fourteen

The day after Lee Harvey Oswald got shot dawned cold and damp, the sky a heavy dark grey that completely hid any trace of the sun. Mom was still in bed when I left for school. I knocked on her door but she muttered that she was sleeping, so I didn't go in. I walked to school alone, not backtracking to Allan's to pick him up even though it was my turn.

School that day felt like the longest six hours of my life. Allan and I didn't say a word to each other all day, and every time I looked at him I felt a pang of guilt about telling him to go to hell. Not that he hadn't deserved it. He'd been a jerk. Still, the thing about Allan was, he didn't ever mean to be a jerk. Richard was a jerk but he *chose* to be a jerk. With Allan, it was like he couldn't really help it.

As soon as the bell rang and set us free, I ran all the way to Kate's. I rounded the corner and slowed to a stop in front of her house. I hesitated before knocking softly on the door. I felt suddenly shy.

Kate flung open the door. "Ha. You came."

"I said I would, didn't I?"

"Yeah, but I thought you might just be saying that to get me off your case."

I gave her a small grin.

"Ha! You smiled. You know you hardly ever do that?"

"I smile plenty."

She rolled her eyes. "Whatever you say, Jack. Come on in."

I stepped inside. I could hear music playing. I recognized it right away: Frank Sinatra. The house smelled like spices—not cinnamon or baking spices but something peppery.

"You must be Jack"—Kate's mom stepped into the front hall—"Kate's new friend."

She was very tall—almost as tall as my dad—and she had the same hair as Kate, dark and curly. You could tell it'd be as wild as Kate's, too, if she didn't have it cut so short. "Nice to meet you," I said, " Mrs...uh..." I realized I didn't even know Kate's last name.

"Levine." She grinned.

"My mom likes this music." I realized as I spoke that I hadn't heard music in our house for the longest time.

Mom used to always have music playing: Perry Como, Eddie Fisher, Patti Page. She liked old music mostly, music from when she and Dad first met. Not Elvis Presley. She didn't like him at all.

"It's wonderful music, isn't it?" Mrs. Levine began singing along. "*The dreams I dream, only the lonely dream...*" She had an amazing voice, deep and gravelly.

"Mom," Kate said. "Please."

Mrs. Levine broke off, laughing. "Am I embarrassing you, darling? Come on in, Jack. I'll make hot chocolate and we can get to know each other."

Kate's kitchen had a black-and-white–checkered floor, red chairs around a small, chrome-legged table, and shiny white cupboards. It was much bigger and brighter than the kitchen at my house. It was also much messier. Dirty dishes were stacked by the sink, pots covered the stove top, and a half-played Monopoly game took up most of the table. "Just push everything over," Mrs. Levine said. "Clear some space for yourselves. Careful with the game though—I have hotels on Mayfair and Park Lane."

"Go ahead and jiggle it," Kate said. "Swipe me some money while you're at it. My mother is merciless." She got mugs out of the cupboard while Mrs. Levine put a saucepan of milk on the stove.

"Only way I can get my daughter to drink her milk," Mrs. Levine said. She didn't sound like she minded though.

I slid the Monopoly board over, clearing a patch of smooth yellow tabletop. Kate put the mugs beside the stove, rummaged in the cupboard and handed a tin of Carnation hot chocolate to her mother. I stood there watching them both and feeling awkward.

"So, Jack." Mrs. Levine stirred the milk slowly with a wooden spoon and looked at me. "Kate was telling me your mother's been having a hard time."

She made it sound so ordinary somehow. "Yes, Mrs. Levine. That's right. For a while now." I put my hands into my pockets and quickly took them out again. Dad said it was bad manners to stand with your hands in your pockets.

Mrs. Levine stopped stirring and turned to face me, leaning back against the stove. "Kate told me about your little sister. I'm so sorry about your loss, Jack."

"Thank you."

Kate pulled out one of the red vinyl chairs, sat down and motioned for me to sit beside her. I sat down gratefully. She winked at me.

Mrs. Levine tucked a curl of hair behind her ear. "So tell me about your mom. What's she like?"

"Now, you mean?" I shrugged. "Most days she doesn't even get out of bed."

"I mean before all this. Underneath it, Jack. What is she really like?"

I looked up at the ceiling. "Um, she used to laugh a lot. I used to like making her laugh. And she liked music. Dancing. Cooking. Sometimes she and Dad played bridge with the Millers." I chewed on my lip. "She liked singing."

"Oh, I love singing," Mrs. Levine said. "So does Kate. She plays recorder too—you should hear her."

"Mom! Jack doesn't care about that."

"No, that's okay—I mean, that's great…"

Mrs. Levine smiled at me before turning back to the saucepan. "Oops, I'm going to burn the milk. It's sticking to the bottom of the pan." She stirred ferociously, still talking. She talked every bit as fast as Kate. "So, Jack, has your mom seen a doctor?"

"Yes. He gave her some medicine."

"Hmm. Has it helped?"

I frowned. Dad wouldn't be happy if he knew I was talking about this, but there was something about Mrs. Levine that made talking feel easier than it had in a long time. "I don't think so," I said honestly. "Back in the beginning, after Annie died, she cried a lot, but that kind of made sense, you know? And she still *talked* to me. But now…" I shrugged. "Dad says she's sad, but she doesn't seem sad exactly. More…I don't know—like she's given up. Like she's not feeling much of anything. She sleeps all the time."

"Hmm," Mrs. Levine said again. "Does she talk to anyone?"

I shook my head. "My aunt came and stayed for a few weeks last fall, but things are worse now, really. And Mrs. Miller used to visit her sometimes, but she hasn't been over for a while. I don't think Mom really wants to see her anyway."

"She should talk to someone," Mrs. Levine said. "Where do you live?"

"335 Church Street," I said.

"Hmm." Mrs. Levine had a look on her face that reminded me of Kate.

"Dad wants her to see the doctor again, but she doesn't want to."

"Doctors," Mrs. Levine muttered, stirring so vigorously that milk sloshed onto the stove. "Sometimes I think they're overrated."

Kate giggled. "My dad's a doctor."

"Really? He is?" I didn't know why, but I was surprised.

"Not that kind though. He doesn't talk to people or anything. He's an X-ray doctor."

"Radiologist," Mrs. Levine said.

"Oh. Right. I wish my mom had the kind of problem that would show up on an X-ray, you know? A broken leg, say, or a dislocated shoulder." I broke off, realizing how that sounded. "I mean, not that I want my mother to break her leg…"

"I knew what you meant," Mrs. Levine said. She dumped a big scoopful of hot-chocolate powder into the milk and stirred. "Those kinds of problems are a lot easier to fix, aren't they?"

I nodded. "It doesn't seem like anyone knows how to help my mom."

"Sometimes you can't," Mrs. Levine said. "Sometimes all you can do is keep on loving someone anyway, and make sure they know it."

I looked down at the table, blinking, unable to speak. My throat was closed up so tight it hurt.

"Maybe I'll pay her a visit. You think she'd mind?" She filled two mugs and carried them over to the table. "I'll let you add your own sugar. Don't go wild."

"Oh, I won't. I mean, it's already sweet enough."

She grinned at me as she put the sugar bowl on the table. "It's not you I was worrying about."

Kate wrinkled her nose. "I have a sweet tooth."

Mrs. Levine changed the record, putting on a Perry Como album I recognized from home. Kate and I sipped our hot chocolate in silence. I ran one finger around the rim of my mug and licked the chocolate off my fingertip. Kate and her mom were great, and it was nice of Mrs. Levine to say she'd pay Mom a visit, but I couldn't really see how that would help. Not if Dad and the doctors couldn't.

Perry Como was singing "Till the End of Time" and my eyes were stinging. I swallowed hard. "This is my mom's favorite song," I said. "It was the first song she and my dad danced to."

"That is so romantic," Kate said. "Isn't it, Mom?"

"It is." Mrs. Levine sat down opposite me and started singing along. "*Till the end of time…long as stars are in the blue…*" Her eyes were half closed and her mouth was wide open; she sang loudly, as if she was on stage. It was kind of weird, since we were just sitting in her kitchen, but I had to admit she was good. She sounded like a real singer.

"Mom…" Kate pleaded.

"I don't mind," I said quickly. "I wish I could sing like that."

Mrs. Levine broke off in midsentence. "Of course you can."

I shook my head, laughing, then yelped out loud. Kate had grabbed my knee so hard that I practically fell out of my chair. "Ow! What are you doing!?" I pulled away, glaring at her.

"I just had the *best* idea." Kate's eyes were wide, her cheeks pink.

"What?"

"You. You learn to sing that song for your mom. I bet she'd love that. Way more than seeing you eat seventeen sausages. Definitely more than you slapping your friend's face for three days." Kate's words spilled out like cars piling up in a freeway accident. She talked so fast she was hard to understand. "Don't you think so, Mom? If it was you, wouldn't you love that?"

Mrs. Levine frowned. "Jack slapped his friend for three days? What are you talking about, Kate?"

I shook my head. "Uh, no. Thanks, Kate, but I don't think that's a good idea."

"It's better than good, Jack. It is a truly great idea." She turned to her mom. "It is, isn't it?"

"I really can't sing," I said. "I think I'm tone deaf."

Mrs. Levine actually made a noise that was almost a snort. "I doubt that."

"I didn't really slap anyone," I said. "I mean, I did, but he agreed to it. We were trying to break a record." I didn't want her to think I went around hitting people.

"Hmm."

"To cheer my mom up, you know? It used to make her laugh."

Mrs. Levine nodded. Her eyes were like Kate's: dark brown, with long, thick lashes. "Would you like more hot chocolate, Jack?"

"No, thank you."

"What about me?" Kate protested.

"Enough," Mrs. Levine said. "I saw how much extra sugar went into that mug. More like syrup than milk."

Kate sighed. "Jack?"

"Yes?"

"It really is a good idea. Don't you think?" She put her hands on the table, palms down, and leaned closer to me. "Picture this, okay? Your mom is lying in bed, maybe half-asleep, and she hears something. Music! Someone's put a record on, she thinks. Then she realizes it's her favorite song. She listens more closely. Yes, definitely her song…She can hear those words she loves. *Till the end of time*, blah blah blah, whatever the words are." Kate's eyes opened wide, like she was actually living this whole scene in her imagination. "But wait! That isn't Perry Como's voice! She sits up, curious. Who can it be? She swings her legs over the side of her bed, stands up shakily, opens her bedroom door—"

"Okay, Kate. I think we've got the picture." Mrs. Levine gave Kate a warning look.

Kate ignored her. "She walks down the hallway, following the music. And there, in the living room, she sees her own son. Her son, who loves her so much—"

I cleared my throat. "Only one problem, Kate. I really can't sing. I mean, I'm even worse at singing than I am at baseball."

"Everyone can sing," Mrs. Levine said serenely. "And Kate, you could play your recorder. You've been neglecting your practice lately."

Kate wrinkled her nose. "So boring, practicing. Anyway, I think it would be better if it was just Jack."

I narrowed my eyes at her. "Jack isn't doing it at all," I said. "Jack can't sing."

There was a long silence. I could feel both Kate's and Mrs. Levine's eyes on me. My ears were on fire. I cleared my throat. "I should get home," I said. "Mrs. Levine, thank you for the hot chocolate."

"You're very welcome, Jack. It was good to finally meet you. Kate's been talking about nothing else."

"Mom." Kate's cheeks were pink.

"Sorry, darling. Jack, do come and see us again."

I stood up. "Thank you."

"Don't let my daughter boss you into doing anything you don't want to do," she said. "Her enthusiasm gets the better of her at times, but we do both understand how hard a time this must be for you all."

"Yes." I shifted my weight from one foot to the other. "Thank you, Mrs. Levine."

She smiled and tucked a stray curl behind her ear. "I used to teach singing," she said. "And Jack? I meant what I said: everyone can sing."

Fifteen

Mom was up when I got home. She was in the kitchen, staring into the refrigerator.

"Hi, Mom," I said.

She turned and looked at me. "Jack. How was school?"

"Fine. It's nice that you're up."

"I thought I should make dinner," she said. "But I don't know what."

"I can make spaghetti," I offered.

She gave me a tired smile and sat down at the kitchen table. "Thanks, Jack. This medicine the doctor's given me...I feel like sleeping all the time."

"Maybe you should stop taking it," I said. "If it's not helping."

"Maybe." She ran her fingers through her hair, smoothing the tangles. "I'm sorry I'm being so useless."

"Don't say that." I pulled a box of spaghetti from the cupboard and filled a saucepan with water. The kitchen clock ticked loudly. "Mom? Would you like me to put a record on? Some music?"

She shook her head. "I don't care."

"Perry Como, maybe? Or Frank Sinatra?"

"Whatever you like, Jack." She stood up. "I think I'm going to lie down for a few minutes. I've got a bit of a headache."

"Oh," I said. "Okay."

"Thanks for cooking," she said. Her eyes were suddenly shiny.

"I don't mind," I said. "I like doing it."

Mom turned away quickly, but not before I saw a tear escape from the corner of her eye.

I heard her bedroom door close and pictured her crawling back into the mound of covers on her bed. I didn't understand. All of us were sad about Annie, but it had been almost a year since she had died. You couldn't go on forever being sad all the time. Lately there were whole days that I didn't even think about Annie. Sometimes I felt bad about that, like maybe I was forgetting about her, but I couldn't help it. Anyway, it was better than just staying in bed all the time.

Mom seemed like she had gotten lost in something that was way beyond sadness. Like something inside her had broken. I wiped my nose on my sleeve and dumped the spaghetti into the saucepan even though the water wasn't boiling yet.

Singing. Sometimes, when I was little, Mom and I would sing together. She'd put on a record and we'd dance around the living room. This was when I was maybe six or seven, before I started thinking about whether or not I could sing, before I decided I was too old to dance with my mother. Even Allan used to love it. Mom would take each of us by the hand and swing us around, and grab us and tickle us and we'd escape, giggling…I shoved the memory away. It was so hard to connect those pictures in my mind with the person Mom had become.

I thought about what Mrs. Levine had asked—*What is she really like? Underneath it all?*—and realized it had been a long time since I'd thought about who Mom used to be. Was that other version of Mom still there, buried somewhere deep inside? And if she was, would I ever see her again?

Mrs. Levine and Kate had been kind, but I didn't see how they could really help. Kate's idea about me singing seemed kind of crazy. I wasn't even sure my mom would get out of bed if she heard me singing. Maybe she'd just pull the blankets over her head and go back to sleep. Even if she did get up, what would that accomplish? It wouldn't fix whatever was broken inside her.

On Tuesday I walked to school alone again. Allan didn't show up until lunchtime. We were all sitting at the long table in the lunchroom when he walked in. He hesitated, looking at the empty seat beside me and sucking on his bottom lip. He held his orange lunch box in one hand, his matching thermos in the other. Everyone brought their lunch in brown paper bags except Allan. There was something so goofy about him standing there with his shirt buttoned up right to the collar, his hair freshly combed. He looked a bit lost, and before I could reconsider, I gestured to him to join me.

"Dentist appointment," he muttered to me as he slipped into the seat beside mine. "That's why I'm late."

I didn't say anything. I hadn't decided if I was talking to him again or not.

"Sorry," he mumbled. "About what I said."

I couldn't even remember exactly what he had said, but I could remember my reply. "Me too," I said. "Sorry I told you to go to hell."

He nodded. "It's okay. Sometimes I say stuff that comes out wrong. I probably sounded like a jerk." His mouth was slightly open and he was tapping his lower lip over and over again with one finger. "Still frozen," he said, seeing me looking at him. "From the dentist." He motioned toward his lunch, sitting on the table in front of him. "I can't even eat. The dentist said I might bite my cheek or something."

I studied my sandwich, pushed it aside and pulled two Oreo cookies out of my lunch bag. "So, I met this girl—" I started to say.

"*You?* You met *a girl*?"

I shook my head. "Not like that. She's—her name's Kate."

"What do you mean, *you met a girl*? Where did you meet her?"

I didn't want to tell him about my tree house. "Out walking. She just moved here."

"Huh. Really." Allan looked a bit offended. "You never told me."

"Well, now I'm telling you, okay?"

"Huh," he said again.

"Don't get all—huffy."

"I'm not *huffy*."

"Yes, you are. You're sulking."

Allan eyed my cookies. "Can I have one of those?"

"I thought you weren't supposed to eat."

"I'll be careful."

I slid one toward him. "I'm going to her place after school."

His face fell. "Oh. I thought maybe…" He broke off. "Never mind."

I hesitated, not really sure I wanted to share Kate, but Allan looked so disappointed. "You want to come?" I asked. "She wouldn't mind."

"Okay," Allan said. "As long as you don't make me do anything crazy. No more records." He popped the whole cookie in his mouth and chewed slowly. The frozen side of his mouth didn't move much. He looked like he might start drooling.

"No records," I promised. It seemed like everyone I knew was tired of my record attempts. I still thought it'd be cool to be the best at something, but at the same time, it was kind of a relief to give up trying.

On our way to Kate's, I filled him in, telling him about her inviting me over to meet her mother. "She and her mom had this crazy idea. To help my mom feel better, you know? She thinks…" I laughed. "She thinks I should sing to her. One of those old songs she likes, you know?"

To my surprise, Allan looked thoughtful.

"I know it's crazy," I said quickly. "I mean, it wouldn't change anything."

"I don't think it's crazy. Kind of weird, maybe, but you've done plenty of weirder things."

"Oh come on, Allan."

He shrugged. "I know it won't…well, it won't *fix* her. Still, it would be a nice thing to do."

Something else Mrs. Levine had said slipped into my mind. *Sometimes all you can do is keep on loving someone anyway, and make sure they know it.* I walked in silence for a few minutes, listening to the sound of the leaves crunching under my feet. Mom knew I loved her. Not that I said it all the time, like I did when I was little, but she knew. Still, maybe I should think about Kate's idea.

"Too bad you're such a lousy singer," Allan said.

I turned up the driveway to Kate's house. "Kate's mom says everyone can sing," I told him. I knocked on the door and heard a series of thumps from inside—Kate flying down the stairs two at a time. I was grinning even before the door opened and revealed a pink-cheeked, wild-haired Kate.

"Hi," I said. "I brought my friend Allan. Is that okay?" I gave her a look meant to convey both hopefulness and an apology.

"'Course it is. Come on in."

We unlaced our boots and left them on the mat by the door, and Kate took our jackets. "My mom's getting groceries, but she'll be back soon. So are you two in the same class? I wish I was going to the same school as you."

I'd assumed she would be joining us in January. "You're not going to Memorial? How come?"

"Mom says there's another school closer."

"Oh yeah. C.H. Bray." It was a newer school, a low brick building near the rail trail. I'd walked right past it on my way to Kate's house, but it hadn't occurred to me that she'd be going there. "That's too bad."

"We'll see," Kate said. She hung our jackets on a tall wooden coatrack. "It's not as though I mind walking. I walk everywhere. Yesterday I walked to Spring Valley arena. You know where that is, right?"

"Of course I do." I made a face. "I used to play baseball there. My dad was the coach."

"Cool." Kate's eyes were wide. "I wish my dad played baseball. All he plays is violin. Actually, anything with strings. And piano, of course."

"Too bad we can't trade," I said. "Not that I want to play violin, but anything would be better than baseball. I hate baseball."

"How can you hate baseball? I love baseball. You should see me pitch. I'm a great pitcher. Come on in. You want a glass of juice or something?"

I shook my head. "I'm fine."

"What kind?" Allan asked. "Because orange juice makes me a bit nauseous. My mom says I have a sensitive stomach."

"Oh, that's not good." Kate ducked her head and winked at me before turning back to Allan. "Apple juice?" she suggested, with no hint of amusement in her voice.

"Thank you," Allan said. "That'd be great."

We followed Kate into the kitchen and she poured Allan a glass of juice. We stood awkwardly for a minute. The Monopoly game appeared to be still in progress, and there wasn't a free inch of space on the table.

"Let's go in the living room," Kate said. "More comfy." She led the way into a large sunlit room and we followed her, padding in our socks across the soft orange carpet. Kate flopped onto the couch—robin's egg blue. A television stood on a low stand opposite the couch. It was even bigger than Allan's. The room looked like something out of a catalogue, with everything brand-new and modern-looking. I sat down beside Kate.

Allan remained standing, looking around. "Wow," he said. "That's some piano."

"I thought you hated piano," I said.

"I like *playing* it," he said. "I just don't like having to practice every day when I'd rather be doing other things."

Kate looked at him. "You can play piano?"

"I've been taking lessons practically since I was born." He walked over to the piano and ran a finger along the keys. "Do you play?"

She shook her head. "I can, but I don't. I used to take lessons, but I hated it."

"Do you play anything?" Allan asked.

"Recorder." She made a face. "Badly. I'm the only person in this family who's not some kind of musical genius."

Allan played a quick scale. "I'm not a genius, but I'm pretty good."

I didn't understand how he could say things like that without blushing. I nudged Kate's foot with mine, trying to catch her eye, but she ignored me. There was a faraway look in her eyes.

"I have an idea," she said.

Allan stopped playing and turned to face us. "About what?"

She looked at me. "Can I tell him?"

I thought I knew where she was going. "Is it about me singing to my mom? I already told him."

"Are you going to do it?" She jumped to her feet. "It's a good idea, don't you think, Allan? I bet his mom would love it."

He nodded. "I think it's a great idea. I told him I thought he should do it."

Kate grinned. "And you should accompany him, Allan."

"I'm not that good," Allan said hastily.

"We don't have a piano," I objected. "And it'd have to be at my house because, well, Mom doesn't go anywhere."

Kate pursed her lips. "Hmm." Then she clapped her hands together. "Dad's accordion! If you can play piano, I bet you could play that. What was the song, Jack? The one she likes best?"

"'Till the End of Time,'" I said. My voice came out husky, and I cleared my throat. "Perry Como. You know the one?"

She was already flipping through the records. "I have it." She put on the record, lowered the needle and waited. "Listen. This is it, right?"

I listened to the opening music, waiting for Perry Como's voice to sing the first words of the song.

"Ah. You're thinking about doing it then, Jack?" Mrs. Levine was standing in the doorway, unwrapping a long scarf from around her neck, bags of groceries at her feet.

I jumped up. "Let me help you with those bags."

"Thank you, my dear, but I can manage." She sang a few words aloud. "*Long as there's a spring…a bird to sing…*"

"Mom," Kate said. "Please."

Mrs. Levine laughed. "I hope Kate's offered to accompany you on her recorder."

"Actually, no," Kate said. "But this is Jack's friend Allan. I thought maybe he could borrow Dad's accordion and accompany Jack on that. It's sort of like a piano, right?"

"Well, I suppose so. Sort of." Mrs. Levine looked amused. "Nice to meet you, Allan. You'd be welcome to use the accordion. It isn't getting much use these days. My husband loves it, but his work is rather all-consuming."

"I didn't agree, though. I didn't say I'd do it." Allan's cheeks were pink. "I mean, I'd like to help your mom, Jack, but I'm not sure this is a good idea."

"You were sure enough when it was just going to be me singing," I said. The whole situation suddenly struck me as funny: Allan trying to get me to sing, Kate trying to convince him to play an accordion, Mrs. Levine trying to get Kate to play her recorder—all for my mom, who didn't know anything about any of it. In the old days, I could have told her about this, making it into a funny story, and she would have laughed and laughed. "I'll do it," I said suddenly. "I'm a lousy singer, but I'll do it…"

Kate and Allan started to clap.

"On one condition," I went on. "You two both accompany me. Recorder and accordion. I don't care how bad you are—you can't be worse than me."

They both stopped clapping rather abruptly. Perry Como sang on alone: *I'll go on loving you…*

"Well?" I said. "Are you in?"

They looked at each other. Kate looked at her mother. Then she looked at me. "We're in," she said.

"Don't I get to decide for myself?" Allan asked grumpily. "You can't answer for me, you know. I don't even know how to play an accordion."

Kate turned to him and raised her eyebrows. There was a moment's silence. "Oh all right," he burst out, his cheeks flushing brighter still beneath his freckles. They were closer to scarlet than pink now. "I'll do it too."

Sixteen

For the rest of that week and all of the next one, the three of us met as often as we could, which meant that Kate and I met every day after school, and Allan joined us whenever his mom would let him.

"I've told her why I need to see you both," he said. We were sitting around Kate's living room, eating apple slices and cubes of cheese that Mrs. Levine had cut up for us. "She says that's all the more reason I shouldn't skip piano lessons."

"You *told* her?" Kate grabbed her hair, clutching a wild handful in each fist. "Allan! It'll spoil everything if she tells."

"Not that," he said. "All I told her was that I was learning to play the accordion. I thought she'd be pleased. I even told her your mom is a music teacher." He shrugged. "Sometimes I don't understand my mother at all."

"That makes two of us," I said. "I don't understand my mother either."

"My mother's not really a music teacher," Kate said. "She used to teach history at a university."

I stopped, an apple slice halfway to my mouth. "Wow. Really? Why isn't she now?"

"I don't know exactly." Kate shrugged. "Back when I was a little kid, she wrote something the government didn't like."

"So?"

"So she lost her job."

"No way." Allan looked skeptical. "That doesn't make sense."

"Lots of her friends lost their jobs," Kate said. "It wasn't only her."

I hadn't realized Mrs. Levine was listening from the kitchen, but she appeared in the doorway. "Kate…"

Kate looked up and her face flushed. "Mom."

Mrs. Levine was frowning. "No need to drag up the past."

"I just wanted to explain that you weren't really a music teacher," Kate said.

"Did you really lose your job because of something you wrote?" Allan asked.

"Those were difficult times," she said. "Everyone so terribly paranoid about Communism, people spying on their friends and accusing their neighbors…" Her voice was quieter than usual, and although it was Allan who had asked the question, she was looking at me as she spoke. "That's why we left the States."

"That must have been hard," I said awkwardly.

"It was," she said. "I loved my work. And I loved my country too, though some people seemed quick to doubt it."

"That's awful." I looked at Kate for help.

"Yeah. I was only a kid, but I remember it," she said.

I tried not to smile: she said it like she wasn't a kid now.

"We were lucky, compared to many people we knew. But I didn't cope very well, I'm afraid. Not for a couple of years." Mrs. Levine looked at me, her face serious. "Still, I'm fine now, Jack. Hard times don't last forever."

I wondered if she had stayed in bed all the time like my mom did. It was hard to imagine. "Do you think you'll ever go back to the States?" I asked.

"We talked about it, when Kennedy was elected. It seemed—well, it was exciting. Hopeful." She sighed. "I still can't believe he's gone."

"So now…" I wasn't quite sure what I was asking.

"Canada is our home now," she said. "So. How's the song going?"

"Not so great," I admitted. "I've learned all the words, but…"

"The accordion's great," Allan said. "And I've been practicing the song on the piano at home, so I know it pretty well."

"Kate? I haven't heard you practicing much." Mrs. Levine tilted her head and watched her daughter.

Kate shrugged and didn't answer. She was frowning so hard that her eyebrows almost met in the middle.

"What is it? Kate?"

"I stink, that's what." She scowled at her mother. "Allan just picked up the accordion and started playing it like he'd played one his whole life. He's missed half our practices, but he's the best of all of us anyway. It isn't fair. And Jack—well, he says he can't sing, but he sounds fine to me."

"But Kate…" Mrs. Levine leaned forward, holding out a hand to her daughter, but Kate pulled away.

"I'm going to wreck the whole song! My recorder sounds horrible!" She was almost shouting.

"S'true. It actually sounds exactly like this raccoon I saw get hit by a car a couple of weeks ago," Allan put in cheerfully.

Kate whirled on him, and for a second I thought she might hit him.

"He doesn't mean to be a jerk," I said. "He can't help it."

"What do you mean?" Allan looked bewildered. "I was agreeing with her."

Kate looked from him to me to her mother. We all held our breath. Then Kate let out a long sigh. "He's right. It's horrible. I hate playing the recorder."

"It's a lovely instrument," her mom said. "And so portable. You'll be able to play it anywhere you want."

"But I don't want to play it anywhere at all," Kate said. She was turning pink, and her eyes looked suddenly wet. "I know it's really important to you, Mom, but I hate it."

"Important to me?" Mrs. Levine looked startled. "Why would I care?"

"Because. Because you're like Allan: you can play anything. Dad too. And you're always telling me to practice, practice, practice."

"Because I thought you wanted to learn." Mrs. Levine ran her fingers through her hair, which was now sticking out around her head in crooked little spikes.

Kate sniffed and rubbed her hands across her face. "Well, I don't."

"That's fine."

"Really?"

"Yes, really. I don't know where you got the idea..." She broke off. "We can talk about this later. You have company."

Kate turned to us as if she'd just remembered we were there. "Sorry."

"It's okay. You want to sing with me instead?" I asked.

"Maybe." She gave a hiccupy laugh. "Or I'll think of something else. Maybe I could be an announcer. You know…" She put one fist below her mouth as if she were holding a microphone. "*And that was the one and only Jack Laker accompanied on the accordion by Allan—* what is your last name, anyway?"

Kate kept on with her announcing, and as I watched her, I couldn't help thinking how she'd been so sure her mom wanted her to play recorder, and it turned out she didn't really mind at all. Parents were so hard to figure out sometimes.

My mom didn't seem to be getting any better. She hardly ever got out of bed before I went to school, but some days when I got home I'd find her up and dressed, making dinner. Even on those days—her good days—she didn't talk much. When she did, it was in a slow, flat voice, as if it took a lot of effort to get the words out. And most days she just stayed in her room.

I hadn't told my father about my plan. For one thing, it all seemed rather silly and embarrassing when I tried to put it into words: *Me and my friends are practicing a song for Mom.* For another, he'd probably tell me not to bother her.

"Jack?" Kate nudged me.

"What?"

"What did you think? Was that okay? Can I be the announcer?"

"Sure, if you want."

"Because I know you don't really like singing and you're doing it anyway. I don't want you to feel like I'm abandoning you." She bit her lip, waiting.

"No, it's fine. It's a great idea." I hadn't wanted to hurt her feelings by saying so, but the recorder really had sounded pretty awful. "I don't mind the singing as much as I thought I would." It was true, too. The first time I'd had to sing in front of the others, I'd been so nervous I thought I might throw up, but Mrs. Levine had sung along with me and it had been all right. Now I could sing the whole song by myself, and while I was no Perry Como, I secretly thought I sounded pretty darn good.

Mrs. Levine smiled. "There, didn't I tell you? Everyone can sing."

"So, when are we going to do it?" Allan asked. "I mean, you know the song now. And I don't want to brag, but I'm pretty good on the accordion. What are we waiting for?"

"This weekend!" Kate jumped up and down. "Let's do it this weekend."

I hesitated. "I don't know."

"Tomorrow?" Allan suggested.

"Not when my dad's home." I looked at Mrs. Levine. "He always tells me not to bother her."

"Hmm." That was all she said, but she looked as if she wanted to say more.

"What?" I asked.

"Nothing." She looked at her watch. "Goodness, four o'clock. I should get dinner started. I thought I'd make pork chops, Kate. Your favorite."

"Mine too." There was a lump in my throat, and I swallowed hard. Pork chops. Mom used to make pork chops. Pork chops with mashed potatoes and peas, and chocolate pudding for dessert. *Your favorite*, she used to say, kissing me on the top of my head as she served the food.

"You're welcome to stay, Jack." Mrs. Levine smiled at me.

I shook my head, thinking. Dad wouldn't be home until five thirty. There was time. "We could go to my place. We could do it right now."

"Now?" Kate's eyes were wide.

"Now," I said.

Seventeen

The three of us walked to my house, Allan carrying Kate's dad's accordion in its hard grey case. It was cold and already getting dark, and a light drizzle was falling.

"Are you nervous?" Kate asked. "Because I am. I hope your mom doesn't get mad."

Anything would be better than staying in bed all day, or wandering around all blank and silent, like a ghost. "She won't get mad," I said. I didn't think she had the energy for anger.

"I haven't been to your house," Kate said. "Isn't that strange? You've been to my house lots of times."

"That's it there," Allan said, pointing. "With all the fence boards stacked up against the wall, see? His dad's building a bomb shelter." He glanced at me apologetically. "Oops, sorry. That's a secret, isn't it?"

"Neat," Kate said. "I won't tell anyone."

"My house is much bigger," Allan said. "I live on Hillcrest. Down near McNiven's farm, you know?"

Kate nodded. "I play in the woods there sometimes." She winked at me as we walked up my front path, and I knew she was thinking of our tree house and that she knew, without either of us saying so, that it was our secret.

"Shh," I said, taking out my key and opening the door. We tiptoed into my house and took off our shoes and coats. I couldn't hear any sounds from the kitchen, and my mom's door was closed. I pointed down the hallway. "She's in her bedroom," I whispered. "Come on."

Allan and Kate followed me into the living room. My heart was racing, but when I turned to look at the two of them, I almost started to laugh. They both were wide-eyed, shuffling their feet nervously. Allan was clutching the accordion, still in its case, to his chest; Kate was chewing on her bottom lip. I didn't think I'd ever seen either of them look nervous before.

"What are you grinning about?" Allan whispered.

"Nothing. Are you guys ready?"

Kate nodded. "I think I should announce you after you sing," she said. "So your mom hears your voice first. Otherwise it might scare her, you know? If she thinks other people are in her house?"

"Okay." She had a point. "Allan, are you ready?"

He knelt, unbuckled the case and lifted the accordion out carefully. "Sure, I guess so."

I took a deep breath. "One…two…three…" My eyes met his. "Allan?"

"Yes?"

"Thanks."

He smiled. "'Course," he said. "We're friends, right? Anyway, I like your mother, Jack. If my talent can help her…well, I'm happy to share it."

I grinned at him. "Then let's do it." I took a deep breath and listened as Allan put his fingers on the keys and played the introduction. Then I closed my eyes, pictured my mother standing in front of me and began to sing her favorite song. "*Till the end of time, long as stars are in the blue…*" I thought of her singing it, dancing with my father. I thought of how he used to bend her backward and kiss her, like they were movie stars. I thought of how she used to dance me and Allan around the living room. I thought of her sitting on the couch, rocking Annie in her arms, singing to her.

Tears were sneaking out from beneath my closed eyelids, but I kept on singing and my voice stayed steady, right until it broke on the final words: "*I'll go on loving you.*"

When I opened my eyes, my mother was standing in the doorway, wearing her housecoat and slippers. "Jack?"

"Mom." My throat closed up and I couldn't speak.

She held out her arms and I ran to her, my chest aching.

Mom folded me in her arms and I buried my face against her shoulder. "Look at you," she whispered. "You've grown. You're almost as tall as I am."

I hadn't noticed it, but she was right. I wondered when that had happened.

"That was Jack Laker, singing Perry Como's 'Till the End of Time,'" Kate said in her announcer voice. "He was accompanied by Allan Miller on the accordion. And that song goes out to Jack's mother, Marion Laker, whom he loves very much indeed." Her voice cracked. "We hope she enjoyed it."

Mom's arms tightened around me. "I did," she said softly. Then she let me go and looked at my friends. "Hello, Allan. I didn't know you played accordion. I'm impressed."

He grinned. "Thank you, Mrs. Laker."

"And I haven't met your friend," Mom said, looking at Kate. "Hello. You must be Kate. I'm sorry, I'm not even…" She gestured at her housecoat.

"That's okay. I wear pajamas all the time when I'm at home."

"Your mother has been to visit me a couple of times," Mom said, smiling at Kate. "So kind. You look so much like her."

I hadn't known Mrs. Levine had actually come to see my mother. No one had told me, and I felt thrown off balance by the news. "Her mother taught me to sing," I said.

"It's nice to meet you," Kate said politely.

"Let me get dressed," Mom said. "Jack, your father will be home soon. Would you three be up for an encore?"

I grinned, feeling like my heart might burst. "Yes," I said. "Of course."

Eighteen

When my mother came out of her room fifteen minutes later, she was wearing the same old yellow dress and cardigan, and even though she'd taken so long in there, she hadn't put on lipstick or even brushed her hair. I felt a flicker of disappointment. For a minute I'd let myself imagine her miraculously restored to her old self, but obviously that wasn't going to happen because of one song. It had been stupid of me to think it might.

"Well," she said. "I suppose I had better make dinner." She smiled at me, but she sounded tired, as if the thought of preparing a meal was completely overwhelming.

Kate cleared her throat. "Let us do it," she said. "I'm not a bad cook."

"Won't your family be expecting you home for dinner?" Mom asked.

"Yeah," Allan said. "Your mom's making pork chops, remember?"

Kate ignored him. "I make great spaghetti with tomato sauce. Do you have spaghetti?"

"I think so." Mom hesitated. "But I should do it."

Kate grabbed Allan's arm. "We love cooking," she said firmly. "You and Jack should sit down."

The two of them disappeared into the kitchen, Allan muttering something about not really knowing how to cook. I turned to look at my mother. "So. Um… did you want to sit down?"

She followed me to the couch and took a seat. "Your friend doesn't take no for an answer, does she?"

"Tell me about it," I said, sitting down beside her. "She probably can cook though. I think she can do most things."

"That was sweet of you. The song, I mean." She put her hand on my knee and gave it a squeeze. "Your father and I danced to that at our wedding."

"I know." I stared at my feet, digging my toes into the carpet.

"Jack, I know I haven't been much use lately." She grimaced. "It's been hard."

"I know. It's okay."

She shook her head, and I could see tears starting in her eyes. "It's not okay. I haven't been much of a mother to you, have I? I'm sorry."

"It's okay," I said again. "I just wanted to do something nice for you. I didn't mean to make you feel bad." I looked at her. "Please don't cry."

"I know I've been selfish." She twisted her hands together in her lap. "I'm sure it's been hard for you and your dad too."

"Mmm." Sometimes I wondered if Dad and I were the selfish ones. We'd been able to go on with our lives without Annie. "I'm sorry about all the dumb stuff I did. Trying to break a record, I mean. I thought maybe it would help somehow. Cheer you up, or make you proud of me. But it didn't work, and I kept making Dad angry."

She tilted her head and studied my face. "Oh, Jack. Your dad just worries. Anyway…" She smiled—a real smile, the kind that came with a little breathy sound that was an almost-laugh. "I think you did break a record."

I looked at her doubtfully. "What record? World's worst Perry Como imitation?"

She laughed for real at that. Then she put her arm around my shoulders and kissed the top of my head. "World's best son," she said.

Kate and Allan emerged from the kitchen just as Dad pushed open the front door.

"Dinner's ready," Kate announced.

Allan looked at me. "Are we going to sing for your dad?"

"I guess." I stood up. My legs felt all trembly and I wasn't sure if it was because of the conversation with my mother or the prospect of singing in front of my father.

Allan didn't give me time to chicken out. He picked up the accordion. "One…two…three…here goes, then." He began playing the introduction as my dad walked in.

"Marion?" Dad stopped dead. He opened his mouth as if he was going to say something, then shook his head and sank down beside my mother on the couch.

Allen shot me a sideways look but kept playing. My heart was racing, and when I started to sing, my mouth was so dry I could feel my tongue clicking. The first few words were flat, and my voice sounded to me as if it was coming from somewhere far away. Then I caught my mother's eyes and she smiled, and my voice was suddenly my own again, and I kept singing. "*Long as there's a spring, a bird to sing, I'll go on loving you…*"

It wasn't until the very end of the song that I looked at my father. I think part of me was afraid he would be scornful—that he would think singing was a bit of a sissy thing for a twelve-year-old boy to be doing—and another part was afraid he wouldn't understand why I had done it, that he would think I was showing off. But when I sang the last line and finally looked at him, my father's eyes were shining; he was clasping his face with one hand, hiding his mouth. I wasn't quite sure, but I thought he was holding back tears. Allan played the final notes and quickly put the accordion back in its case. He looked at Kate. "Are you going to…"

She shook her head. "Come on. We should get home."

"Thanks," I said to them. "For playing, and for making dinner and everything." I walked them to the front door. "I really appreciate it."

"Yeah, yeah." Allan put his coat on. "She liked it, didn't she? I could tell."

"You sounded great," Kate said. "I didn't want to do the announcing thing again—it didn't seem right, somehow."

"No, that's fine," I said. "I know."

"You sounded pretty good," Allan said. "I mean, you're no Perry Como, but you remembered all the words and everything. She did like it, didn't she? What about your dad? I couldn't tell what he thought. He was kind of frowning, wasn't he?"

I shrugged. "Dunno what he thought."

"He liked it," Kate said firmly. She took Allan's arm. "Come on, Allan. Let's go."

"Bye," I said. They left with shrugs and smiles—all of us were feeling a little self-conscious and uncomfortable—and I waved goodbye. I stood there by the door for a long minute, watching them walk away. I'd never seen my dad cry and I didn't want to now.

When I returned to the living room, Dad was sitting on the couch alone and I could hear the clanking of cutlery and dishes in the kitchen.

"Your mom's serving up dinner," he said.

I shifted awkwardly from one foot to the other. "I should help set the table," I said, backing away.

"In a minute." Dad beckoned to me. His eyes were dry, and I wondered if I had imagined the shine in them earlier. "That was quite a performance you gave."

I shrugged. "We thought Mom might like it."

"She did." He looked at me thoughtfully. "So did I."

I exhaled a lungful of air—I hadn't realized I'd been holding my breath—and met his eyes. "I wanted to do something to help her. To make her feel better."

Dad's eyes were shiny again, and this time it definitely wasn't my imagination. "I want to help her too, but it isn't going to be that easy. She loved your song, and it was very thoughtful of you. But…"

"But it's not going to make a difference."

He sighed. "She's grieving. It's understandable."

"So are you," I muttered. "And you still go to work and everything. You didn't give up."

"Shh. That's enough." Dad looked toward the kitchen. "You'd better go set the table, Jack."

Nineteen

It turned out that Kate couldn't actually cook. Or maybe she'd been trying to give me more time alone with my mom. The spaghetti was so overcooked it was gluey, and the sauce was a heated-up can of chili. Dad wrinkled his nose but ate it anyway. Mom was playing with her food more than eating it, but she always did that these days.

"Your friend Kate seems very nice," she said.

"She is."

"And it's nice to see you and Allan getting along so well." She tilted her head to one side. "I know you haven't always found him easy."

I was surprised that she'd noticed. "He's okay," I said. "That's just the way he is."

Dad grunted. "Pampered." He stood up and refilled his water glass. "Sounded good on that accordion though. Kid's got talent."

"Kate plays recorder, but she doesn't like it," I told him. "She sounds pretty awful, to tell you the truth. I think she was only sticking with it because her mom wanted her to. Well, Kate *thought* her mom wanted her to, but…"

"Sometimes you have to put in the time to get good at something before you start enjoying it," Dad said. "You get out what you put in."

"I guess so. But I'm not sure Kate would ever like the recorder. Sort of like me and baseball." I held my breath.

He just laughed. "You weren't that bad."

"I was." I made a face. "I still am, when we play at school."

Dad took a mouthful of soggy spaghetti, chewed slowly and swallowed. "Well, there are more important things in life than baseball."

"I know *that*," I said.

And of course I knew it. Still, it was good to hear that my father knew it too.

The next day, Mom didn't get up until late, but when she did finally emerge from her room, she looked different. She was still in her housecoat, hair uncombed and tied back, so it took me a minute to figure out what had changed.

"Hey," I said. "You're wearing your necklace. The one I gave you."

Her fingers flew to it. "It's lovely, Jack." She smiled at me. "Thank you."

I was sitting at the kitchen table, doing my homework and eating breakfast cereal. "It looks good on you," I said. "Sparkly."

She opened the fridge and took out a carton of orange juice. "Where's your father?"

I nodded at the window. "Out in the yard. Putting the fence back up."

"Good. Are you going to help him?"

"After I finish this math." I studied her face. It wasn't just the necklace that was different. "You look...you look like you're feeling a little better."

"I decided to stop taking the medicine the doctor's been giving me. Actually, your friend's mother suggested it. Her husband's a doctor."

"An X-ray doctor," I said.

"Well, I thought she might be right. Every time I saw my doctor, he increased my medication, and I was feeling worse and worse. So I started cutting down on it a couple of weeks ago. I'm still taking a low dose, but I'm planning to get off it completely." She poured herself a glass of juice. "I don't think it was helping. It made me feel so tired and sort of numb. I think..." She looked at me. "I want to feel like myself again."

"Even if…well, even if you're sad?"

"Even if I'm sad." She smiled at me. "I'm not all better, Jack, but I'm trying. Okay?"

There was a lump in my throat. "Okay."

Outside, Dad was mixing water into the bags of rapid-set cement he'd dumped into the wheelbarrow. "Can I help?" I asked him.

He nodded at me. "I could use an extra set of hands. You can hold the posts straight in the holes while I pour the cement in."

"Okay." The holes were all ready, and a five-foot-high post lay beside each one. I hefted a post to vertical and lowered it into its hole. "Does that look straight?"

He fished a small level from his tool belt. "Check it. Both ways—back to front, and left to right."

I measured, straightened the pole and measured again. "You want to look?"

"Doesn't have to be perfect," Dad said. "If you say it's straight, that's good enough for me."

I nodded. "It's straight." Dad poured the cement while I held the post steady. "Can I let go?"

"Yup. Let's do the next one."

We worked in silence for a while, moving from post to post down the line, starting by the corner of the house and moving away from it. "About time we got this done,"

Dad said gruffly, as he poured cement into the last hole. "This place has been a mess for too long."

I wondered if he meant just the backyard or more than that. I wondered if he was thinking about Annie. "I can help," I offered.

Dad surveyed the backyard. "Be nice if you could do some weeding."

"I can do that," I said. "No problem." Maybe I could persuade Kate and Allan to do it with me. I'd ask Kate first, because she'd probably say yes, and if Kate and I were doing yardwork together, Allan might help because he wouldn't want to be left out.

Dad pushed the wheelbarrow off to one side, then turned back to me. "Jack. This business with your mother. With her not being well—"

"I know me singing a song isn't going to fix her," I said, my words spilling out in a rush. "I just wanted…I don't know, to do something for her. Something better than trying to break a record."

"Huh?"

"I thought for a while that maybe breaking a record would be good, because it always used to make her laugh. Well, you both did. You used to think it was funny."

He nodded heavily. "Hasn't been much laughter in this house lately, has there? Not much fun for you."

"I'm okay," I said quickly. "You don't have to worry about me."

"You're a good kid, Jack. If you really want to break a record, you'll do it someday. For yourself, not just to make us laugh. Be sensible, though."

I nodded. "No more eggs." I couldn't help grinning. "Or sausages."

Dad's eyes widened. "The other morning? Oh no, that's disgusting." He started to laugh. "I thought you looked a little off, come to think of it. How many did you eat?"

"Six," I admitted. "In one minute."

"What's the record?" He was really laughing now.

"Seventeen."

"Seventeen! Oh my. Oh my…" He chuckled and wiped his eyes with his sleeve. "Well. Well, well, well."

Dad's face was turning red, his eyes watering, and I couldn't hold back my own laughter. Finally he shook his head, sighed and gestured widely at the row of fenceposts, secure in the fast-setting cement. "Well, that's a good job done, Jack. And about time I got that fence back up."

"Mom's getting better, don't you think?" My voice cracked embarrassingly.

"I suspect it'll be up and down. Good days and bad days. But…" He broke off. "I do think she's getting better. I didn't agree with her deciding to stop taking her medicine, but I think she was right after all. She seems more like herself again."

"I guess she must have loved Annie an awful lot," I said.

Dad cleared his throat. "We all loved Annie," he said. "I was thinking about what you said earlier—about me going on with work and everything."

"Sorry," I said. "I shouldn't have said that."

"It's okay. It's true: I did carry on in a way your mother couldn't."

"Me too," I whispered. "I mean, I was upset and everything, but sometimes…" I glanced up at him and then looked away quickly. "Sometimes I felt kind of bad that I kept going to school and having fun with my friends and stuff."

"I know," Dad said. "I know."

I snuck another peek at his face. He looked sad but not upset.

"But if you hadn't carried on," I began hesitantly. "I mean, if you'd *both* gone to bed and stayed there…" I couldn't imagine it, and I didn't want to.

He nodded. "I guess we all have to deal with this in our own ways." He dusted his hands off on his work pants. "As best we can."

I didn't say anything because of the huge lump in my throat.

"Your mother loves you, Jack. Every bit as much as she loved Annie." He rubbed his chin. "She wouldn't want you to stay sad."

"I wish Annie hadn't died," I whispered. "And I wish Mom would get better."

Dad put his arm around me. "She will, Jack. She'll be all right. We all will."

"I know," I said. I leaned my head against his shoulder and breathed in the damp, woolly smell of his sweater. Despite the lump in my throat and the tears blurring my eyes, I felt better than I had in a long time

Twenty

On Sunday, the three of us—Kate, Allan and I—walked over to Tony's to buy candy together. Kate still had the dime she'd found on the floor of the shop. Allan had dumped his piggy bank—an actual piggy bank, pink ceramic, with a red bow tie—and Dad had given me a quarter.

"How much is that?" Kate asked Allan. He was jingling a fistful of coins.

"A dollar," he said. "I'm not spending it all on candy though."

"If I brought all my money, I'd end up spending it," Kate said.

"Me too," I admitted.

Allan put his money into his pocket. "I just want some Tootsie Rolls and maybe some licorice. And some Hot Tamales."

"Oh, that's all?" I asked.

My sarcasm went over his head. "Maybe some candy cigarettes too," he said.

The temperature had dropped and there were heavy banks of cloud hanging low in the sky, piling up along the horizon in layers the color of steel and smoke. "Think it's going to snow?" I asked as we rounded the corner onto Wilson Street.

"Hope so," Kate said. "I can't wait to go tobogganing. Where are the best hills, anyway?"

"Golf course." Allan and I spoke in unison. We looked at each other and laughed. "It's pretty decent," I said. "You have a toboggan?"

"A new wooden one," Kate said. "Got it last Christmas."

I pushed open the door to Tony's. "Cool."

"Hi, kids." Tony was drinking a can of cola, eating peanuts. A newspaper was spread out on the counter in front of him. "What's cooking?"

"We've all got some money for candy," I said. "How are you, Tony?"

"Never been better," he said, winking at me.

I gave Allan a sideways glance—*see, told you there's nothing wrong with him*—but he was distracted by some plastic toy and didn't notice.

"Check this out," he murmured.

"What is it?" I looked closer and read the label on the box: *Blow soap bubbles for fun! For big colorful bubbles use*

Wonder or U-Blow-It liquid! "A bubble pipe?" I shook my head. Sometimes he seemed like such a little kid. "Come on, Allan. Let's pick out our candy."

"I'm getting this too," he said.

Kate laughed. "Told you you'd end up spending that dollar if you brought it all with you."

"Actually, you didn't say that, Kate." Allan pushed his glasses up farther on the bridge of his nose. "What you said was that if *you* brought all your money, *you* would spend it. Which is a different thing entirely."

"Oh, entirely."

Allan looked at her suspiciously, but Kate's eyes were wide and innocent.

"Hey, let's see that bubble pipe," she said.

Allan handed it to her. Kate turned it in her hands, her lips moving as she read the package silently. Her forehead furrowed in concentration, and the tip of her tongue poked out between her teeth.

"What is it?" I asked her.

"I have an idea," she said. "Jack, is there a record for the world's *biggest* bubble?"

"Don't think so." I shook my head. "No, I'm pretty sure there isn't. Not in my book, anyway."

She grinned.

I grinned back at her. "You know," I said, "I bet we could do it. I bet if we added something to the soap, to thicken it, like glycerin, maybe..."

"We'd have to experiment," Kate said.

"Oh no," Allan said. "Oh no."

Kate laughed and handed the pipe back to him. "You're in, right?" she said.

"'Course he is," I said. "We're all in."

Acknowledgments

Many thanks to the BC Arts Council for their generous financial support during the writing of this novel.

Robin Stevenson is the author of many books for teens and children. Her novels have been nominated for numerous awards, including the Governor General's Literary Award and the Sheila A. Egoff Children's Literature Prize. Robin was born in England, grew up in southern Ontario, and now lives on the west coast of Canada with her partner and son. For more information about Robin and her books, please visit robinstevenson.com.